MARRIED FOR THE BOSS'S BABY

BY
SUSAN CARLISLE

MILLS
BOON

Published in Great Britain 2016
By Mills & Boon, an imprint of HarperCollins*Publishers*
1 London Bridge Street, London, SE1 9GF

© 2016 Susan Carlisle

ISBN: 978-0-263-26429-6

Our policy is to use papers that are natural, renewable and recyclable products and made from wood grown in sustainable forests. The logging and manufacturing processes conform to the legal environmental regulations of the country of origin.

Printed and bound in Great Britain
by CPI Antony Rowe, Chippenham, Wiltshire

Susan Carlisle's love affair with books began in the sixth grade, when she made a bad grade in mathematics. Not allowed to watch TV until she'd brought the grade up, Susan filled her time with books. She turned her love of reading into a passion for writing, and now has over ten medical romances published through Mills & Boon. She writes about hot, sexy docs and the strong women who captivate them. Visit SusanCarlisle.com.

Books by Susan Carlisle

Mills & Boon Medical Romance

Midwives On-Call
His Best Friend's Baby

Heart of Mississippi
The Maverick Who Ruled Her Heart
The Doctor Who Made Her Love Again

Snowbound with Dr Delectable
The Rebel Doc Who Stole Her Heart
The Doctor's Redemption
One Night Before Christmas

Visit the Author Profile page at
millsandboon.co.uk for more titles.

To Anna,
I'm glad to call you daughter-in-law.

CHAPTER ONE

Dr. Grant Smythe glanced at the bassinet. His father and stepmother had been in the grave only a day and the nanny had quit. Just walked out. What else could go wrong?

No doubt his father was rolling over in his grave at the idea that Grant had been awarded custody of his baby half-sister. He was pretty sure his father had had no intention of ever telling the child she had siblings.

Grant paced the oak planks in the foyer of what had been his father's home.

Where is the new nanny? When is that woman going to show up?

He checked the time on his phone. She should be here by now. They were waiting on him in the OR. The liver he was to transplant wouldn't be viable much longer.

The baby whimpered. Grant shoved his hair off his forehead. This was just one more of his father's ways of making him feel inadequate. One final sick joke.

The whine grew to a cry. Where was…? *What is her name…? Uh, Sydney, Sara, Sharon or something.*

The baby released a deep-chested, high-pitched scream. What was wrong? He hadn't had anything to do with babies since med school. Even then it had only been for a short time.

Baby. He was so bitter he couldn't even call the small

bundle by her name. Grant looked into the cherubic face twisting up to make another cry. His sister. *Lily.* He shouldn't be taking out lifelong issues with his father on an innocent babe. "Lily," he whispered.

Her mouth closed and she studied Grant.

Amazement filled him. The child was beautiful. She resembled Evelyn so much. Her mother. The same woman he'd once planned to marry. Lily could have been his daughter. At least that was until he had introduced Evelyn to his father. Those were dark thoughts Grant didn't have time for.

The ring of his phone drew his attention. Surely that was the nanny saying she was on her way. Answering, he recognized the voice of Leon, his best friend and lawyer. When Grant had taken responsibility for Lily he'd contacted Leon to watch after his and the child's interests.

Without any preamble Leon said, "Well, it looks like Evelyn's family means business."

"I had no idea she even had an aunt and uncle. She never said anything about them."

"Doesn't matter. They're here now. Maybe you should consider letting them have Lily. What do you know about raising a child? Adoption could be the right way to go. We can set it up so that you oversee her trust fund."

Grant still couldn't get over the fact that a couple had showed up at the funeral saying they were his stepmother's family members. The man had then informed Grant that they were planning to file for custody of Lily.

His sister. His family. She should be with him.

Why he felt so strongly about that he had no idea. Did he still think he needed to prove something to his father? That shouldn't matter. He'd spent most of his adult life fighting with the man. He was gone now. A dejected feeling settled over Grant. No matter how bad it had been between them he still hated knowing his father was gone forever.

Grant look down at Lily. "What do we know about these people?"

"Based on a preliminary report of the Armsteads, they look like the perfect couple to take in a child."

"And I'm not," Grant snapped. "What about the life-style I can offer her?"

"To be quite frank, it won't matter."

"So what would make a difference?"

Leon sighed. "The court likes to see children going to a couple. If you were married it would help your case one hundred percent. You're the closest relative. You have the means and ability to care for her. I don't see a judge, even the most conservative one, going against you."

"So what you're telling me is that I need to find a wife," Grant said flatly.

"In a word, yes."

Sara Marcum still couldn't believe she'd agreed to take this job. She pulled her beat-up car into the curved brick drive of a two-story mansion in Highland Park, the poshest section of Chicago, Illinois. The yard was so manicured each blade of grass stood at attention.

Kim, a nursing friend who worked at the hospital, had called her that evening and told her about Dr. Smythe's desperate need for a nanny. Knowing Sara was available, she'd given her the doctor's address and asked her to go there immediately. The problem was that Sara wasn't nanny material. She wanted nothing to do with caring for a child.

"You have a big heart, Sara, you're just the person to help this guy out," Kim had insisted. "It's just temporary and the money's good."

Currently between hospice nursing positions, Sara

wasn't sure she could return to doing that type of work. She had loved and hated her job. After Mr. Elliott, one of her favorite patients, had died painfully over many weeks it had become too much. When he'd passed away Sara had decided it was time for a change. She needed to get away to recover but couldn't afford not to have any income. The need for her father and herself to eat and have a roof over their heads took priority. Which was the only reason she'd agreed to consider this nanny position.

Her cellphone rang as she drove up the drive. "Hey, Dad."

"We've have a problem, little girl." Sara had long since outgrown the nickname but her father continued to call her that.

"What's wrong now?" She was so tired of fighting off creditors.

"Mr. Cutter just came by. He's evicting us."

She gripped the steering-wheel. "He's what? He can't do that!"

"Well, he is. He has someone who wants the apartment."

"I told him I would get the rent caught up as soon as I could. I paid an entire month just a few weeks ago." She wanted to scream. Would it ever end?

Growing up, she'd known her father had worked hard to make ends meet. After his accident, finances had become ever tighter. He now received disability but nothing else. The company had managed to see that he was blamed for the explosion and had awarded him no compensation. She'd wanted a nursing degree so badly she'd gone into debt to get it. It had taken her years but she had paid her loans off. Yet here she was, trying to survive again.

"I reminded him but he doesn't care. He wants us out by the end of the week."

Sara gave an exasperated sigh. She was tired of moving. Now she had to do it again. But to where?

They had been doing well. She'd had some savings and had even been starting to look into buying a house when her father had answered a telemarketing call. Lonely and at home by himself too much, he had been the perfect victim for a fast-talking salesmen to take advantage of. Before he'd been done, all of her father's money had been invested in land in Florida that didn't exist and most of hers was going to keeping her father's doctor's bills in check. Even with this job she would barely keep their financial heads above water.

"I've got to go, Dad. Don't worry, I'll figure something out." *But what?* She rang off.

She pulled to a stop in front of the house. Before she had completely climbed out of the car a tall man holding a baby tightly to his chest was hovering over her. In his arms the child was but a tiny bundle. "What took you so long?"

Going motionless, Sara held his gaze for a moment. The baby cried out.

"Look, I'm sorry," he said over the infant's wailing. "They're waiting on me in the OR. Can you please just come in?"

He rushed inside the house, leaving the door wide open. The baby's bellows filled the air.

Unable to bear the little one's distress, Sara slammed her car door and hastily followed them. She stopped in the hallway.

The man thrust the babe into her hands. "Will you please take her? I have to go."

Sara grasped the baby with a growing knot in her throat. She'd told Kim she couldn't do this. But she had insisted. Why did every child have to bring back the fear of getting too close? That horrible ache that never seemed to ease. Sara looked into the infant's face. That was a mistake. "Go?"

"I'll be back later," Dr. Smythe announced. "Everything you should need..." he pointed toward the back of the house and up the large staircase "...is in the kitchen or upstairs in the nursery."

"Dr. Smythe—"

"No time." He picked up his keys from the table in the foyer and headed for the open door.

Sara hurried after him and called, "You can't just leave."

"Can't talk right now."

"I don't care if I'm being evicted or not, you're not paying me enough for you to just dump this child in my arms and leave! Come back here."

"We'll go over things later." He was gone. The large door closed with a thump behind him.

Sara stood there in disbelief, looking down at the unhappy child in her arms. He'd handed the baby over with no thought. Nothing like her reaction when, as a surrogate mother, she'd given up a baby. If she'd have been able to, she would have hung on for dear life. But that hadn't been the agreement. She still carried the pain. For her there was nothing cavalier about relinquishing a baby.

What had she gotten herself into? She'd known this wasn't a good idea. But she was here now. Sighing, she had no choice but to see to the baby for the time being. Leaving the baby by itself wasn't an option. Sara would never, ever do that. When the presumptuous doctor returned she would tell him that this arrangement wasn't going to work. She would still need to figure out something for her and her father. Maybe she could make Mr. Cutter see reason. Working for Dr. Smythe wasn't the answer.

Walking across the black-and-white-tiled floor, she entered the living area. It was the most un-child-friendly place she'd ever seen. With overstuffed white sofas and chairs sitting on plush white carpet, she could only hope there was never any red juice in this child's life.

Heavens, she didn't even know if the baby was a boy or a girl, much less its name. The infant let out another scream.

It must be time for a diaper change and a bottle. Then she would put the tyke down for the night. There must be a nursery somewhere but for now the kitchen would have to do. At least she could find some food for the child. If she focused on the practical, maybe she wouldn't need to worry about the emotional part of working with a baby.

Sara gathered what looked like a diaper bag and headed down the wide main hall in search of the kitchen. It turned out to be a wide, spacious room with large windows overlooking a swimming pool. A small house sat beyond. The garden surrounding the area was green and immaculate, like the front lawn. If she had ever imagined a perfect kitchen, this would have been it. She'd heard of the Smythes and their status in the community but to live in this opulence was far beyond what she was used to. The baby whined. Sara jiggled it.

Dropping the diaper bag on a padded bar stool, she walked to the corner area of the room near the table. There she found an infant seat that could be set on the table. She strapped the baby in, leaving the bouncer on the floor while she hunted for formula. Not seeing any on the counter, she checked in the refrigerator. Inside were already prepared bottles. Setting one on the bar, she lifted the baby seat up and, after heating the bottle to the right temperature, started feeding the child.

The baby's angry face turned angelic in its eagerness to eat. At least someone was happy. Something that simple tugged at Sara's heart. What would it have been like to see Emily smile with this kind of pleasure? She had to forget that time. It was gone. But she couldn't forget. Still clung to those precious days.

Grant stretched his arms out, waiting as the surgical tech slipped the green gown over his arms and went around him to tie it in the back. Had he lost his mind?

He knew nothing about babies. Hadn't wanted to know anything about them. Now one had been plopped into his lap. More amazing was that he planned to fight to keep her.

Grant's teen years hadn't been easy between him and his father, but his parents' divorce had made it even worse. His father had left his mother. The breakup had devastated her. She'd taken it so hard Grant had feared that she might be committed. With his parents divorced and his older brother living in a commune in California, all his mother's care had fallen on Grant. Thankfully he had convinced her to get help. Now she was living in Florida and by all accounts doing well.

To strain the relationship further, his father had ended up marrying Evelyn, the girl Grant had been in love with. Even at thirty-two, being betrayed by them had been the final slap in the face Grant had been willing to take. Trust had been hard to regain. His interactions with his father and Evelyn had been few and far between over the last two years. His father had made an effort but Grant had been unable to forgive him. Learning that he and Evelyn had had a baby only disgusted him more.

"Dr. Smythe, they're waiting for you in surgery," another tech called.

Grant shouldered his way through the swinging OR doors and into the room. The patient, a middle aged man, already waited on the table. "Sorry I'm late," Grant said to the room in general before asking the anesthesiologist, "John, is everything ready to go?"

"Patient is stable," John answered.

Grant stepped up beside Jane, the woman who was dressed much as he was. She was just months away from finishing her training as a transplant surgeon. "Where's the liver?"

"Thirty minutes out," Jane answered.

He nodded. Looking at the patient, he could see Jane was already in the process of opening. "Good, then let's get this patient ready to receive his new liver. He has a family waiting."

Here in this OR Grant was in control, the best at what he did. He appreciated order. Outside, life was more difficult, unexpected. Now that his father and stepmother were gone, he had to admit to a tinge of guilt over his father dying with their relationship in shambles. When Grant had learned his father hadn't updated his will after Lily's birth he'd found it difficult to believe. With his brother unavailable, Grant had been the next in line to receive custody of Lily. He couldn't let his newborn sister be taken by state services, could he? How would his father have felt about that? He didn't want to give her up to Evelyn's aunt and uncle either. This was one task he would demonstrate himself worthy of.

"Doctor, the organ is here."

A man entered, carrying a cooler. The pace would pick up and Grant would have to apply all his energy to seeing that the bad liver was removed and the new one put into place. He wouldn't have time to think about Lily.

With the blood vessels clamped off and the organ removed, Grant inspected the new one. "It looks good. Let's get this done." Gently he placed the liver into the cavity and began stitching the vessels to it. The phone of the OR wall rang. Grant continued to work.

"Dr. Smythe, it's for you."

His brow wrinkled. "Who is it?"

The nursed asked, then called, "It's a woman who says she's your nanny."

"What the hell?" he murmured. Louder, he said, "I can't speak to her right now."

The nurse relayed the message. "She is being rather insistent."

He huffed. "Jane," he said to the fellow, "would you please check for bleeding and start closing while I get this?"

A soft mumble followed him to the phone. His colleagues must find the situation curious. It was out of character for him to take a call while in the OR. He had a good relationship with his team but he was also known for not tolerating interruptions during surgeries.

He resisted grabbing the phone out of the nurse's hand. "This had better be good," he growled into it. "I'm in the middle of surgery."

There was silence on the other end. Finally a voice said, "It's Sara Marcum. I'm sorry, I had no idea that they would put me through to the OR."

That eased his aggravation a little. "Now that you have me, what do you need?"

"It's late. Since we had no time to talk I wanted to know if I'm supposed to stay the night. I didn't come prepared for that. I have a father who is expecting me home."

Grant hadn't thought of that as he'd rushed out of the house. He'd just assumed… "Yes, I am going to need you tonight. Every night. If you'll please just make do for now, I promise tomorrow I'll give you a full list of your responsibilities. I need to get back to my case."

"I have responsibilities as well but I'll be here with the baby until you come home."

"Thank you." He hung up the phone. What responsibilities? Could hers be more important than a baby or a lifesaving transplant? He paused for a second. Hadn't she said something about being evicted? Maybe she had gigantic problems as well. He'd get this transplant patient taken care of first and then head for the house. Losing a nanny again wasn't what he needed.

As he returned to the table his team gave him questioning looks over their masks. He shrugged. "I was given custody of a baby and have a new nanny. Now, can we get this patient closed and out to ICU?"

Sara hung up the phone. Dr. Smythe hadn't been happy with her call but he'd left her no choice by leaving so abruptly. With an eviction on the horizon she needed the money this job would bring, but she wouldn't allow anyone to treat her unprofessionally. He had almost done so by all but throwing the child at her and leaving.

It was time to find that nursery. Sara cradled the baby in her arms and, with the diaper bag slung over her shoulder, she climbed the wide circular staircase to the second floor. Going along the passageway, she searched each room for one that looked like a baby's room. At the end of the hall, across from the master bedroom, she found a small slice of heaven.

The walls were painted the palest pink. She'd had a pink room growing up. It had been that color when her mother had left. When this little girl became old enough, would she think she had done something wrong to make her mother leave, as she herself had? She hoped not.

Above a snowy-colored crib draped in rosy colored netting was the name 'Lily' in white letters on the wall. *Lily. Pretty name.*

Sara had been in such a hurry on the phone she'd forgotten to ask Lily's name. It was nice to have one to call her. Sara looked down into the big eyes watching her. The baby looked like a Lily. The disadvantage to knowing her name was that it was another step closer to giving them a personal connection. Knowing someone's name made you care more, the very thing Sara wanted to guard against.

The regal room fit Lily perfectly. Moving across the thick carpet of a similar quality to what was downstairs, Sara placed the baby in the bed.

What had Dr. Smythe been thinking? Only about himself, handing his child over without so much as telling Sara her name?

The medical field was a small world and she'd heard talk about the young dynamic doctor who did surgery with skill and precision. Still, to give your baby to someone you didn't know and rush off without concern spoke of self-centeredness, even neglect. Hadn't her mother done something similar with her? Sara had grown up thinking she'd caused her to leave. No child should wonder something like that.

Locating the diaper stacker on the closed double doorknob, she had Lily changed in no time. Her job as a nursing aide during her school years had been teaching summer help how to change diapers. Back then she'd enjoyed working with babies. Now she usually steered clear of them.

Lifting Lily off the bed with her little limbs flailing, Sara went to the rocker next to a window that looked down over the garden. A large oak limb hung just outside. Every child should have such an idyllic place to live. Sara watched Lily as she placed the nipple of the warmed bottle to hungry lips.

For a brief time Sara would dedicate herself to meeting Lily's physical needs. The emotional ones would be seen to by her father. Sara wouldn't let herself get too close. She was well aware of how hard it was to pull away.

With Lily settled in her crib, Sara chose the bedroom nearest the nursery as hers for the night. It had been an exhausting day and she was soon asleep.

Grant returned to the house around midnight. The surgery had gone well and all he wanted was a soft bed and some sleep. He had spent the travel time out to Highland Park thinking about what he'd have to do to get permanent custody of Lily. Could he marry just to keep her? Some part of him hated the possibility of losing her while the other worried about making such a drastic decision. Was he the best choice to raise her? Would his father be pleased he was taking such an interest in Lily?

The one thing he did know was that he would do a better job than his father had done with him. Lily wouldn't always feel as if she didn't measure up or was unloved if she messed up. She would know she was supported, no matter what.

He'd been on a major adrenaline rush since his father had died. What if he was just making decisions based on sentiment instead of rational thought? Was he thinking he could make his dead father happy by taking care of Lily or was he doing it to get back at Evelyn for treating him the way she had?

It didn't matter what his motive was, he wanted to keep Lily and if that meant taking a wife then he would do it. None of the women he'd dated recently or in the past would fit that position. Even if he could get one of them to agree. They would be more interested in their looks and spending his money than they would be in Lily.

Maybe Evelyn's aunt and uncle were the answer. Lily could have a home, people who really wanted her. But he did too. Was he prepared to devote the next eighteen to twenty-two years of his life to someone other than himself? He thumped the steering wheel with the palm of his hand. Lily should be with him and he intended to fight to keep her, even if it meant he had to marry.

Grant pulled into one of the three bays of the carport in the back of the house. He unlocked and opened the door to the kitchen. Quiet greeted him. There was a light on under the counter. When was the last time someone had left one on in anticipation of his return?

He grabbed a glass from the cabinet and headed to the refrigerator. Taking out the milk, he was in the process of pouring it when the pixie-sized nanny burst into the kitchen, holding an umbrella as if she was prepared for a fight.

Grant jerked upright. Milk spilled across the granite countertop and streamed onto the floor. Grimacing at the mess, he snarled, "Hell, woman, you almost scared me to death."

"How do you think I feel? Waking up in this hulking house to hear a door shut?"

"I told you I'd be home tonight."

"After the way you left, I was supposed to believe you?"

Grant hung his head. He deserved that. His leaving had been rather abrupt. "I owe you an apology." He looked at her. "I'm sorry."

With large brown eyes, her shoulder-length hair in disarray around her face, she captured his attention. She wore the same T-shirt she'd had on earlier and jeans. Most women he knew wouldn't have been caught dead without every hair in place. Not this one.

He cleared his throat. "Why don't you have a seat and we'll talk while I clean this mess up."

"It's late. Aren't you tired?"

"Beat. But I don't know if I can be counted on to be here in the morning." He tried for one of his most charming smiles. "And I don't want to take the chance that you might use that umbrella on me."

She looked at the instrument, as if she'd forgotten she held it, then at him. "Okay, but just for a few minutes. Lily will be awake again soon."

His father and Evelyn had named Lily after his paternal grandmother. Grant had once confided in Evelyn that he wanted to give the name to a daughter one day. He'd trusted her with that knowledge and she'd violated it. It was just another example of how she and his father had cared nothing about his feelings. He'd sworn he'd never trust that freely again. With every woman since Evelyn he'd been cautious about what he revealed about himself. If he didn't let a woman get to know him too well then he didn't have to worry about being hurt by her. Show no weakness.

That had been the problem with his father. He'd used it against him. Grant had wanted to impress him, wanted to do the right thing in his eyes, but nothing had seemed to please him. Grant had worked at it as a kid and even as an adult, hating himself for caring what his father thought but still trying to please. Maybe raising Lily was just one more way of proving he was good enough. Irony. The way to say *I told you so.* He was disgusted with himself. Even with his father gone, he was still trying to demonstrate himself worthy of being his son.

The nanny—he wished he could remember her name—had hung the umbrella on the back of a chair at the table and sat down. She had an expectant expression on her face.

Grant grabbed a dishrag and started mopping up the

milk. What had she told him her name was over the phone? When Kim had called that afternoon he'd been looking for paper and pencil to write it down but Lily had started crying.

Tossing the rag in the sink, he dropped into the chair at the end of the table. "I'm sorry, I can't for the life of me come up with your name."

She raised a finely groomed eyebrow. "Let me get this right. You're not even sure that I'm the person you were expecting? What if I had kidnapped Lily? You couldn't even tell the police my name." She leaned toward him, her voice rising with indignation. "I sure hope you show more concern for your patients."

Okay, he deserved some of what she said but he was a fine doctor and refused to take that comment about his professionalism. "I'll have you know that my patients take precedence with me."

"Yeah, I don't doubt that. I saw an example this afternoon."

He'd walked into that one.

"Let me help you. I'm Sara Marcum. I'm here until you can hire a full-time nanny for Lily. For now she is fed, clean and sleeping upstairs." She stood. "It's late. I'm tired. We can continue this discussion in the morning. Good night."

Sara straightened, making the thin shirt material cup her breasts. She wasn't wearing a bra. Her nipples pushed against the fabric. Grant couldn't help but stare.

She made a small sound of distaste and picked up the umbrella. For a second he was afraid that she might really use it on him but she headed out of the kitchen. The view of her backside was almost as inviting as her front. She had a high, firm butt that made her jeans more than just clothing.

Grant shook his head. He had patients to see about and Lily to situate, his father's estate to settle, and now a smart-mouthed, take-charge nanny who was too cute for his own good.

Nope, that wasn't a road he would be going down.

CHAPTER TWO

SARA WOKE FROM a deep sleep. It took her eyes a moment to adjust to the darkness and for her to register the low shriek of a baby. Slinging the covers back, she jumped out of bed.

How long had Lily been crying?

Sara wasn't tuned into the child as her real mother would be. Would she have had that maternal bond with Emily? The question made her flinch. It couldn't have existed in her own mother because it had been so easy for her to leave. She shook away the darks thoughts. Right now Lily needed her.

With no clothes but those she'd arrived in, she was sleeping in her T-shirt. Padding barefoot down the hall and into the nursery, she used the nightlight to see to scoop up Lily. Sara pulled the child against her chest in an effort to quiet her. Despite Sara's annoyance over Dr. Smythe's attitude, she did have compassion toward him regarding his rest. At two months, Lily wasn't quite old enough to sleep through the night yet. She probably had a wet diaper and would soon settle down after her nighttime bottle.

Laying the child back in the crib, Sara gathered what she needed to change Lily. All the while the baby's cries grew. She talked softly, trying to soothe her. Wasn't that what a mother would do? Sara didn't need to think that way. She was halfway back to the crib when a large male form filled the doorway. She groaned.

"Can't you make her hush?" a deep sleepy voice grumbled. Grant stood there like a thundering god with his chest bare and boxers covering his slim hips.

"She has a wet diaper. I'm changing her."

"Good. I have to be at the hospital early." He turned to leave.

Sara couldn't stop the words. "I don't control when Lily wets herself."

He blinked then pushed a wavy lock of brown hair off his face and took a step closer. "Hey, I'm sorry. I'm not being fair. Just do what you have to do. I don't have the time or the inclination to look for anyone else to help me right now. Please try to ignore my sour attitude."

That was more like it. "I'll do what I can but we need to establish some ground rules."

Sara wasn't intimidated by type-A doctors. She wouldn't be walked over by a self-important domineering doctor, or anyone else for that matter.

"I'll check in at the hospital and then we'll have that discussion. Will that be satisfactory?"

"That'll be fine. Now, if you'll excuse me, I'll take care of Lily." She had started toward the baby's bed again. "Oh, by the way…"

He stopped in mid-turn.

"I would appreciate it if you would put some clothes on around me."

He glanced down. "I did."

An O formed on her lips as he walked away.

Grant was dressed in his casual work clothes when he entered the kitchen to the sound of humming. Sara had Lily sitting in her baby seat on the table while she fed her. Lily seemed as enthralled with the nanny as she was with her.

Sara had made a smart comment about his dress last night. What had she expected from a man awoken out of a deep sleep? A tux? She'd had on that T-shirt that showed her full breasts to their best advantage and he hadn't complained. She believed she had the moral high ground and he let her stay there while he enjoyed the view. The woman had something special about her that he couldn't put a name to.

"Hello."

Sara turned, a surprised look on her face. "I hope we didn't wake you this morning."

"I heard nothing. It's time for me to head to the hospital."

She went back to feeding Lily. "You keep long hours."

"That's what happens when you're building a transplant program." He went to the coffeepot and poured himself a cup then leaned a hip against the counter.

"It must be tough to do while taking care of your daughter's needs at the same time."

His chest constricted for a second. He'd not told a soul about his father's betrayal. What should he say? The truth in as few words as possible. It still wouldn't make it hurt less. "Lily isn't my daughter. She's my half-sister."

Sara gaped. "Your sister? How?"

He shrugged his shoulders. "You know, in the usual way. My father impregnated his very young second wife and, ta-da, I have a baby sister."

Her eyes widened. "I had no idea. Kim said nothing."

Grant set his coffee down with exaggerated care. Their gazes met and he said softly, "My father and stepmother both died in a car accident last week."

Her look of shock deepened to one of disbelief. He

didn't doubt her sincerity when she said, "I'm sorry to hear that. I just assumed your wife left... I'm sorry."

"I guess, based on my actions so far, you wouldn't be surprised if my wife had left me. But I don't have a wife. Never have." Had never planned to. *But that was going to have to change.*

Going back to feeding Lily, she said quietly, "I'm sure Lily's parents would be relieved to know you are taking care of her."

He looked away. Maybe they would be, maybe they wouldn't. Either way, Lily was his responsibility now. "I'd like to think so. I just want to make sure I do the right thing by her."

"I'm sure you will."

He didn't miss the catch in her voice. "You can tell that I need help. I can't see about Lily and be gone all the time." He gestured helplessly. "You've already seen what it's like for me." Why did he feel the need to prove himself to this virtual stranger?

"I understand." Somehow the sympathy in her voice made him feel better. Sara gave her complete attention to the wiggling child in front of her. "Not everyone is cut out to be a parent. All you can do is your best."

What did she know about that? He liked the idea that in the end he might please his father by keeping Lily. To feel like for once his father was proud of him. His throat constricted. Surely he wasn't looking for a dead man's admiration. He would need to give that ugly idea additional thought.

"I have to change her." Sara picked Lily up and headed out of the room.

If he didn't get going he would be late to work. He wasn't used to extra people in his world first thing in his morning. Not even women he dated were allowed to stay overnight at his apartment. Since his father's death his life had been swirling out of control. He was responsible for a baby. Not just any baby but his sister. Now he had a perfect stranger sharing the same house as well.

Sara placed Lily in her baby swing, pleased the child was so easy to care for. If not for her fears of getting too close and the unpredictable Dr. Smythe, she might come to like this job. And that was what she was afraid of.

Then there were the moments…like last night when Grant had stood in the doorway half-naked in front of her as if that was all right, or when he'd left the house without a fare-thee-well this morning while she'd been upstairs with Lily that skirted close to arrogance. After all, they were strangers. His behavior made her question the wisdom of staying. Where did the man get off treating people the way he did? What had happened to common courtesy?

Once he returned she'd find out how long she was expected to stay and when she would be paid. She had to start looking for a place to live right away. Meanwhile, when she finished her job here she could decide if she wanted to return to hospice work or look for a different nursing position. Either way, she had her father to think about. Somehow she had to find him a nice safe home.

After lunch, Sara put Lily down for her nap. The child was a beauty. She looked like an angel sleeping. Sara walked away from the crib. Grant would have to find another nanny soon.

She went to the den she'd discovered at the back of the house. With its dark paneling, bookshelves, hardwood floors and overstuffed chairs and couch, it was a perfect place to curl up for some downtime. She settled into the corner of the couch, the baby monitor nearby and the TV on. It wasn't long before her eyes slipped closed.

Heavy footsteps coming down the hall woke her, announcing that the doctor was home. She had just put her feet on the floor when he appeared in the doorway. From the entry, his look circled the room and came to rest on the desk. His expression was one she couldn't quite put a name to but it came close to pain. He seemed to have forgotten that she was there. Where had his mind gone? After a few moments his attention focused on her.

"Let's talk in the front room." He didn't give her time to answer before he turned and stalked back down the hallway.

What was wrong with him?

Dr. Smythe was pacing before the formal white brick fireplace when she entered the living room. As she sat on the edge of a chair, he turned and placed an arm on the mantel, looking down at her. Was he trying to intimidate her? It was too late for that.

He cleared his throat. "Again I want to apologize for the abrupt way I left yesterday but it couldn't be helped." There was a pause. He must have seen her skeptical lifted brows. "I had a patient waiting in the OR. I appreciate you coming to care for Lily on such short notice."

"Dr. Smythe, Kim said you only needed me until something permanent could be arranged. How long do you think that will be?"

"Call me Grant. After all, we'll be living in this house together…" he looked around with what she could only describe as disgust "…for a while. And I'm not sure how long I'll need you."

Living here longer than a few days? With him? Holding, feeding and caring for Lily? A breath caught in her throat. Panic filled her chest. She couldn't get stuck doing this job. The greater the time she spent around Lily the more difficult it would be for her to let go. Sara was well aware of how she would react. It was her nature to get too close to people. And painfully aware of how difficult it was to give up a child.

He must have seen her reaction. "Look, I know we got off on the wrong foot but the other nanny left me high and dry and I needed someone right away." He moved to sit in the chair closest to her. Placing his elbows on his knees, he leaned toward her. His intense dark gaze held hers. "I'm grateful that you were able to step in. I can already tell you are great with Lily. I would really appreciate it if you could be flexible."

With his pleading eyes and his calm clear voice, Grant was making it hard for her not to agree. He was a man desperate for help and admitting it. Something she suspected he rarely acknowledged. Could she keep her emotional distance from Lily for however long he needed her? On top of that she would be living with a stranger, and an attractive one at that. When had her life become a soap opera storyline?

Sitting back, he watched her. "I understand you're a hospice nurse."

"I am."

His hands rested on the arm of the chair. "Tough job. Takes a special person to do that kind of work."

"It's rewarding."

Now he was playing the charm card. He was desperate. In any other situation she doubted he'd be interested in her. She wasn't his type. He was more of the glossy, statuesque and glamorous woman kind of guy while she was the homey, girl-next-door person. Outside of Lily and medicine, she was pretty sure they had little in common.

"I imagine it can be emotionally draining."

"It can be." She didn't want to talk about it. With a sigh, she said, "I'll agree to two weeks. No more."

"Excellent." He smiled then stood, returned to the fireplace and looked up at the portrait of a beautiful young woman. Sara assumed it was Lily's mother.

"What're my duties?"

"I just expect you to take care of Lily."

Sara relaxed on the couch. "Having no idea I would be a live-in nanny, I brought no personal things with me."

"Feel free to buy what you like. I'm glad to pay." His tone implied that his thoughts were somewhere else.

He must be kidding. Who gave a woman carte blanche for clothes? "I'll ask my father to pack me a few things. Could you send a delivery service to bring them here?"

"Give me your address and I'll take care of it."

"Thank you. I'll also need to have Saturdays off."

He glanced at her, his face holding a stricken look. "I'll work something out."

"Am I to be responsible for seeing to the house and food as well?"

Grant appeared perplexed as if the thought had never occurred to him. "Uh, there's a housekeeper who comes in once a week. Please handle the groceries and supplies for yourself and the baby. You're welcome to have it all delivered. I'll put some money at your disposal."

"Thank you. I'll be sure to keep a record of how it's spent."

"I'll be in and out, mostly out, and I'll leave all that to you. If you need anything and can't reach me, just contact my assistant." He fished a card out of his slacks and handed it to her. "By the way, there's a car at your disposal in the garage behind the house. It already has a car seat in it. The key is hanging beside the kitchen door. You can pull your car around and use the bay next to the black sedan. I have to get back to the hospital." With that statement he disappeared out the door.

Sara needed to call her father and let him know the arrangements. That she would not be home for a couple of weeks. When she had spoken to him last night he had sounded concerned about her staying at a stranger's house but understood her need to remain there with Lily. Now, on the phone, her father sounded sad.

"Sara, you shouldn't have to be doing something you really don't want to. It's my fault we're in this position. You should be living your life, having your own family, instead of caring for someone else's child and worrying over my stupid decisions."

She winced at the words *your own family*. That might never be possible. "We've talked about this before and I don't want to hear any more about it. We're in this together. Anyway, everything is going to be all right. I'll find us somewhere to live. Enough about that. Daddy, would you please pack a few things for me in a bag for the next few days?"

"Sure, little girl."

Sara gave him a list. "A delivery service will come by to pick the suitcase up."

"I'll have it ready."

Grant arrived back at his father's house well after dark. The front porch light was on. He pulled his vehicle into the bay beside Sara's.

A light was on over the back door and one shone in the kitchen. Sara was a considerate woman. He entered through the kitchen door. His intention was to go straight to bed but a piece of paper on the counter caught his eye. In clear penmanship was written, "Please let me know when you come and go. I like to know when someone is in the house."

He'd been accountable to himself for so long that he'd

never even thought to say anything when he came or went. Crumbling the note into a ball, he tossed it in the trash before starting toward the stairs. In his room he emptied his pockets and kicked off his shoes. Walking through the bathroom adjoining his and Sara's bedrooms, he found Sara's door closed. It would be his guess that she'd had no idea that they shared a bathroom when she'd picked this room. He tapped lightly on her door. No response. Rapping again, he listened and then opened it. Light shone across the floor. Sara looked small in the large bed with only a sheet covering her.

"Sara," he called in a low voice. He didn't want to startle her but she had asked for notification when he arrived.

"Um…" She twisted toward him, giving him a glimpse of firm behind covered in hot pink panties.

When Kim had told him she knew someone who could help him, he'd assumed it would be an older female. Not a pretty young woman. Being attracted to the nanny hadn't been part of his plan. That didn't make him much better than his father. No woman off limits. With a sick feeling he categorized them both as lechers. The one person he had no interest in being like was his father.

"Sara," he called again.

She sat up part way.

"I'm home," he almost growled.

Instead of a T-shirt she wore a nightie with spaghetti straps. The delivery man had apparently brought her clothes. As she turned, the material tightened, giving him a glimpse of the curve of a breast.

He couldn't do this nightly. His libido would get the better of him. Neither did he need to chase her off. The rapport between them was tentative enough as it was. He desperately needed a nanny and he couldn't have her backing out on their agreement.

"Oh. Okay. Thanks for letting me know."

"Sure." The hallway door was the closest and his fastest escape. From now on he'd come home well before bedtime or leave a note on the door.

Over the next three days Sara spent the time feeding, changing and cleaning Lily. While she did so she made sure she didn't hold Lily any longer than necessary. The more she looked into the sweet face or played with Lily, the more Sara knew it would be increasingly difficult to leave her when the time came. She wasn't going there again. The first time hadn't ended well. Giving up Emily had been too hard.

Keeping her emotional distance was her goal. She only had a few more days to go. If she could earn enough for a down payment on a place to live and keep her heart uninvolved, she would consider it a job well done. Even now she feared she might have some trouble leaving Lily when the time came but she would do it. She'd done it before and would do it again.

She wasn't having the same problem with Grant. Despite all the time she'd spent with Lily, she'd only seen Grant a handful of times. They had said one or two words to each other and he had been out the door each morning, and after that first day he'd not even picked up Lily.

Except for the one night he'd awakened her he hadn't stayed at the house. She'd checked the master bedroom each morning and the bed hadn't been slept in, but he'd been in the kitchen dressed and ready to go when she and Lily had come down. Surely he wasn't spending that much time at the hospital.

Sara hadn't bargained on sleeping in the huge house by herself and she didn't like it. She needed to speak to Grant and see what the deal was. He was probably staying out at night, having a good time with a woman. Did he have a girlfriend? What if he did? Why would she care? It was none of her business.

He never asked about Lily or ever really had any interaction with her when he was home. It was as if he was afraid to have anything to do with the child. Was he purposely making sure he didn't become fond of her because he was worried he might lose her?

Early Wednesday morning the house phone rang. Sara didn't bother to pick it up. The answering-machine would get it. From where she stood at the kitchen sink she could hear the message.

"Mrs. Smythe, this is the children's clinic, calling to remind you that Lily has an appointment at four o'clock today with Dr. Gomaz for her two-month checkup. Please call if you won't be there."

Why hadn't Grant told her about the appointment? Didn't he know she should be informed of those sorts of things? He shouldn't have custody of Lily if he couldn't handle the details of her life.

Mrs. Smythe couldn't make it but Sara would see Lily was at the appointment.

By that afternoon, Sara had to admit that getting a baby fed and dressed on a deadline was not for the meek and mild. Just strapping one in a car seat was a feat in itself. She had started just after breakfast and she was going to have to hurry to get to the appointment on time. It didn't help that she was driving an unfamiliar car. At the hospital where the children's clinic was located, she drove around and around the parking structure, finally locating a space on the top level.

Sara worked Lily out between the parked cars. Removing the stroller from the rear, she was glad she'd had the forethought to bring it. It was unbelievable that one small child was so difficult to handle. Sara smiled. The old say-ing about walking in a man's shoes to know what he re-ally did was true.

She managed to get to the doctor's office just minutes before the appointment. Thankfully the wait wasn't long. Soon Lily's name was called. The doctor pronounced her healthy and said she needed a shot. After that the smil-ing nurse gave it. It hurt Sara almost as if she'd been the one the needle had been used on. Tears came to her eyes. She cuddled the crying Lily close, softly reassuring her.

Still holding Lily, she pushed the stroller out to the checkout window. A sick feeling hit her. She had no way of paying. She'd forgotten to ask Grant about an insurance card. There wasn't enough money in her personal account for her to cover the cost of the visit.

"Can you just bill Dr. Grant Smythe?" she asked the receptionist.

"I'm sorry but payment is due at time of service."

"I'm the nanny. Can't I make some kind of arrange-ment?" Why hadn't she'd thought this trip through?

The woman shook her head.

Hot with embarrassment, Sara said, "I need a moment to make a call." Putting a squalling Lily in her stroller, Sara found her phone and located Grant's number. She touched it and waited for the call to go through. The longer it rang, the more troubled she became that Grant wouldn't answer.

The exasperated "Yes?" on the other end both startled and relieved her.

"It's…" she glanced at the receptionist "… Sara. I'm sorry to bother you but I'm at the children's clinic—"

"Has something happened?" His voice filled with con-cern, catching her off guard.

"No, Lily is fine. She had a checkup today. They ex-pect to be paid."

There was a deep sigh on the other end of the phone. "You needed an insurance card."

Lily let out an unhappy bellow.

Sara covered her ear. "What?"

"What's wrong with her?" Grant's louder voice filled her phone.

"She had a shot and she's sleepy." Sara tried hard to contain her irritation.

"Do you have enough money to pay?"

"No. I just bought groceries and this isn't just a co-pay. Since I have no insurance card, they expect me to pay the entire bill."

"I'm coming right over." The connection was broken.

Sara sat in the waiting room, trying to calm the crying Lily, grateful that the hospital was just next door.

Ten minutes later in walked Grant dressed in his blue scrubs with his bright white lab coat pulled over them. He wore black clogs on his feet. All the women in the room stopped what they were doing to look at him. He really was a striking male. It wasn't that he was glossy cover model handsome as much as he had a commanding presence. He radiated a vibe of being in control. His rich dark hair, intense brown eyes and tall physique made him attractive, but his mystique was what held women spellbound. Including her. She gulped.

Grant stalked to the reception window and spoke quietly to the woman, who smiled up at him like a sap. He indicated Sara and Lily. Minutes later he joined her. "Okay, that's settled."

"Thank you." Sara stood. "Now, just one more thing."

Grant looked as if he couldn't be bothered.

Sara held out Lily. "Please hold her while I go to the ladies' room."

It took him a moment before his hands slowly circled the whimpering baby's chest. Lily's feet dangled.

Didn't he know how to handle a baby? It didn't matter. He was going to have to hold Lily at least for a few minutes.

CHAPTER THREE

GRANT HAD AVOIDED moments like this since he'd been given guardianship of Lily. Handling her made him think that this could have been his child. Instead it was his father's. The father Grant had never measured up to or been good enough for, except where his girlfriend had been concerned. And his father had stolen her.

Lily whined. He pulled her to his chest and patted her back. She quieted. He was thankful and fairly sure the others in the waiting room were too. He observed Lily's bright eyes surrounded by her peach-colored skin. A soft coo bubbled from his half-sister's lips. Her hand found his pinky finger and circled it.

He may have had a poor relationship with his father and stepmother but he wouldn't betray this tiny being, as he had been. He was obligated to her, to give her what he hadn't had from their father. Even if Evelyn's family won custody, Lily would have his support. She would grow up knowing she had a brother she could depend on. Someone who believed in her.

"You must be a wonderful father," commented a woman with graying hair, interrupting his thoughts. She sat beside a young mother. "Your wife is lucky."

"I'm…" He didn't say any more. It wasn't worth the effort to explain.

Minutes later, Sara returned.

"Okay, I'll take her now."

Before he could hand Lily over the woman spoke up again. "You should have seen your husband in action. Your baby stopped fussing the second he held her close."

Sara looked at him with wide, questioning eyes as if she was surprised. "She did?"

"She did." It gave him an inordinate amount of satisfaction to say that.

Sara smiled at him. "It's not so hard to do if you want to."

Was she referring to him holding Lily or stopping her from crying or both? Apparently Sara had noticed how he'd managed to get around having much interaction with his sister.

"Would you like me to take Lily now? I'm sure you need to get back to work."

The note of hope in Sara's voice that he would need to hurry back to work irritated him. To his astonishment, he said, "I'm done for the day and I'm hungry. Why don't we go to a little café around the corner and get some supper?"

"With Lily?" Sara's look of surprise was almost comical.

"Sure. Parents do it all the time. I think two intelligent adults can manage a two-month-old for an hour. You did bring a bottle, didn't you?"

"Yes, but…"

He started to hand Lily to her but the baby began to cry again. He brought Lily back to his chest and she stopped.

"I guess you'd better carry her." Sara didn't turn fast enough to hide her disappointment. It was as if it hurt her to have Lily prefer him over her. Was she that insecure?

Left with no choice, Grant headed out the door and into

the hallway with Lily happy in his arms. He led the way outside, across the bricked park area and down the sidewalk.

"By the way, did you know that Lily had a doctor's visit today and just forget to tell me?" Sara asked.

"No. How did you know about it?"

"There was a reminder call on the house phone."

He shifted Lily to his other arm. "I looked for a calendar but Evelyn wasn't very good at details, except when it came to her makeup."

"That sounded a little harsh. You get a pass this time for not telling me, but the new nanny needs to have some notice when Lily is supposed to be somewhere. And provided with an insurance card."

"Noted."

She followed him down the sidewalk, pushing the empty stroller. "I've laughed at people carrying a child while pushing a stroller. Now I understand."

Grant gave her a wry smile. Lily was getting heavier in his arms. "It does look ridiculous. The café is just down this way." When they arrived at the glass-fronted eatery he held the door open for Sara. "Let's take that table in the back. We'll be out of the way."

Sara parked the stroller beside the table. "Is she asleep?"

"I think so."

"Let me see." She went up on tiptoe and looked into the crook of his arm. The top of Sara's head was just inches away. She smelled of roses. Was it a scent she wore or her shampoo? Whichever, it was nice. He inhaled deeply.

"She is," Sara declared. "Let me take her. I'll put her in the stroller."

"I can do that." What had gotten into him?

"Okay. Let me lower the seat so it's flat. Hopefully she'll sleep until we get home."

Home. Sara was calling his father's place home. It

wasn't home to him. The only reason he was staying there was because of Lily. His apartment was a bachelor's pad and he liked it that way. Truthfully, he hadn't really felt at home anywhere since he'd been a child. What he remembered about his father's house was that it was where his mother had cried and begged his father not to leave her. His brother had already been living in Idaho, leaving Grant alone to deal with his parents' decaying marriage.

If he gained permanent custody of Lily he'd need to find a new place. He'd have to make arrangements for her to have a good place to grow up. Or could he get past his feelings about his father's home enough to live there? Over the last few days it hadn't been memories keeping him away but the young woman sitting across from him.

"Excuse me, what?" Sara had said something, bringing him back to where he was.

"I wanted to know if you came home last night. I waited up to talk to you but it got late."

"No, I went to my apartment."

"It would have been common courtesy to call."

He met her gaze. "Do you always say what you think?"

"Not always."

Was she holding back her thoughts about him? "I didn't make it home until one and I didn't think you'd want me to call that late."

She gave him a keen look. Was she implying he hadn't even thought to call?

A college-age waitress came to their table. "Hi, Doc, I haven't seen you in a while."

"Hi, Karen. I've been a little busy of late."

"You never said anything about having a wife and baby, Doc. Cute."

"Thank you. What would you like, Sara?"

Sara gave him another look, her eyes narrowing. She

had a way of making him uneasy. His father's look hadn't held that much censure. Grant shifted uncomfortably. Did Sara suspect he'd flirted with the girl?

"BLT and water. Thanks," Sara said, with a smile at Karen.

"And I'll have a Reuben with a soda, please."

"It'll be out right away." The girl smiled at him then looked down at Lily sleeping soundly. The waitress shook her head slightly. "You learn something new every day."

He looked at Sara. Her unreadable gaze held his.

"It's too hard to explain about our relationship, I know. I'm sorry all of this has happened to Lily. To you." She sounded truly sympathetic. For once he appreciated it.

"It's more about Lily. My father and I never really got along."

Sorrow filled her eyes. "Still, you must be grieving on some level. He was your father after all."

Grant didn't like to think about it. He shrugged. "The S.O.B. made my life, my mother's life miserable yet there's something about knowing I'll never see him again that does bother me." How could Sara's simple questioning and earnest looks make him say things he wouldn't tell anyone?

She drew imaginary figures on the tabletop with the tip of her finger. "There must have been some good times."

Grant gave that idea some thought. Had there been? Before the divorce? Had the later years overshadowed everything he could remember about his father?

She continued to draw. Without warning, she looked up and volunteered, "I would miss my father if he died. He's the only family I have. He raised me. If anything happened to him I don't know what I would do."

Did he miss his father? He'd been so wrapped up in Lily, the funeral, estate affairs and his anger, he'd not had time to think about his real feelings. He didn't want to contemplate those now. "What about your mother?"

"She left us when I was four and I haven't seen her since."

"Not even heard from her?"

"Nope."

As horrible as his relationship had been with his father, at least he'd had two parents. He and his mother had remained close. Even though she lived out of state, he still talked to her weekly. "I'm sorry."

"Nothing to be sorry about. It's just the way it is." Did Sara take everything that came into her life with such matter-of-fact acceptance?

"So, have you always lived with your father?" He didn't usually take the kind of interest in a woman that warranted that type of question.

A worried looked formed on her face then disappeared. "Yes. He's disabled. There was an explosion at work years ago and he was hurt."

What had that look been about? Why was he asking all these questions about her personal life? He never involved himself in a woman's life beyond what was required for a good time. His rule was not to make any commitments other than the one to his mother. He didn't trust his judgement of women. The less they knew about him the smaller the chances of him being hurt. He didn't need to know this stuff for her to care for Lily. Perhaps the sharing-a-meal idea hadn't been his wisest.

"Have you found a nanny to replace me?"

He didn't look at her. "No."

"Have you looked? My time will be up soon."

Grant met her gaze. "I thought I could maybe talk you into staying a while longer."

She slowly shook her head. "That wasn't our agreement."

"I know. But I need your help. Don't you need the money?"

Her face turned red and she looked away.

"You said something about being evicted the other day. If you will stay, I'll make it worth your while."

"It won't matter. My father has to be out by this Saturday."

"So where do you plan to go?"

"I don't know. I've not had time to look for anything. I guess to a hotel until I can find us a place."

The waitress brought their food and left.

"Anyway, you have enough to worry about with Lily. This is my problem and I'll handle it."

She was making it pretty clear she didn't want to talk about it any more. He needed to figure out some way to at least get her to stay a little longer.

They ate in silence. Grant had completed his meal and Sara was still working on hers when Lily stirred.

"Do you mind giving her a bottle while I finish?" Sara asked, pulling one out of the bag hanging on the stroller.

"Won't she wait?"

Sara's look implied he had to be kidding. "Yeah, for about three seconds and then she'll cry loud enough to break the windows. What's the deal about holding her anyway? You did a good job earlier. It's just a bottle. She does all the work."

"I guess I could."

"Thank you. I'll be done here in a minute. Then I'll change her diaper and we'll get out of your hair."

"You're not in my hair. I told you I was finished for today."

"You're sure acting like we are."

Sara was starting to annoy him. "Well, you're not."

"That's the way it sounded to me." She placed the bottle on the table in front of him as if she was daring him to admit he was afraid to feed Lily.

"It did not." He was reluctant but had no plans to admit it.

Sara laughed and the sound rippled through him, almost a caress. "We sound like high-schoolers."

Grant grinned. His life had been so serious for so long it was nice to smile. "Rather silly ones at that." He lifted Lily out of the stroller and cradled her in his arm. "Okay, this is my first baby feeding. What do I do?"

"Just put the bottle to her lips and she'll handle the rest."

Grant did as instructed and Lily quit crying the second she had the nipple. He beamed at Sara as she finished eating.

"I told you. Nothing to it."

Lily had finished her meal and Sara stood. "Let me have her and I'll take her to the restroom for a burp and a diaper change. If you don't mind, would you push the stroller out?"

Sara reached down, again coming close enough for his senses to appreciate her, and took Lily into her arms. She did so with complete confidence. It was hard not to trust her. Something he never did where women were concerned. "This baby stuff comes natural to you, doesn't it?"

A startled expression mixed with regret crossed her face. "I learned most of what I know from babysitting as a kid."

Grant watched them go. It was the perfect maternal picture. They could be mother and daughter.

As in Lily's mother.

A wife.

Sara had said she was being evicted. If he offered her a place to live, would she consider marrying him as a business deal? Kill two birds with one stone? The idea was too crazy. But Leon had said that he needed to be married if he stood a chance of keeping Lily. Desperate people did crazy things. What would he lose by asking her? The most she could do was slap his face and quit.

He'd have to give the idea some thought.

Sara washed the bottle she'd used to feed Lily. It was hard to believe she'd been working with Lily and living with Grant for almost a week. Soon she would be on her way. She and her father would rent a trailer on Saturday and move their belongings to a cheap hotel down the road from the apartment complex and then spend what was left of the day looking for another place to live. It made her tired just thinking about what was ahead.

Grant would have to take care of Lily or find someone else to for the day. That wasn't her worry. She needed some time away from Lily anyway. Maybe all the packing she had to do would take her mind off how much she enjoyed being a mother to the baby.

The outside kitchen door was unlocked and to her astonishment Grant walked in. He carried two bags of Chinese food. Other than the meal they'd shared at the café, he'd shown little indication that she and Lily existed.

He placed the bags on the table. "I thought you might like some takeout."

It was thoughtful of him and totally out of character from what she'd seen. "I like Chinese."

"Great."

She put Lily in the windup swing nearby. "I'll get us something to drink. Is tea okay?"

"Sure."

Grant had pulled white cardboard boxes out of the bags and placed them on the table by the time she returned with their glasses.

"Chopsticks or fork?" he asked.

"Chopsticks."

He nodded. "I'm impressed. Never mastered them."

Was the man making an effort to be congenial? She could learn to like this person. "A surgeon who can't handle two sticks?"

"Give me a scalpel and let me loose."

"We can't all be good at everything." She took the offered chopsticks.

"No, I guess we can't."

Was he thinking of his father's expectations of him? She watched as he placed a fork-load of food into his mouth. He had a nice mouth. Full and generous. There were lines around it as if he laughed often. Despite the couple of uncomfortable personal moments between them, he seemed at ease with who he was.

"I'm glad you made it home early."

He shook his head. "This isn't my home. I have an apartment downtown. We're only staying here because this is where Lily's stuff is."

"Okay. I can tell that's a sore subject."

Between chews he said, "You sort of have a smart mouth, don't you?"

She shrugged. "Some people might say that. Hey, since I have you here I have a couple of things I need to discuss. First, I need some cash to pick up a few things for Lily. And the other is to remind you that I will be off on Saturday." A stricken look came over his face as if he suddenly felt sick. She quickly added, "I told you this earlier in the week."

"I remember. I'll take care of Lily. Meet me in my father's study after you get Lily to bed and I'll write you a check."

Grant couldn't remember the last time he'd eaten a meal in a kitchen with someone. Either he was out playing poker with colleagues, on a date or at some sporting event. So why had he decided to come home early and bring dinner? *Home.* He hadn't called this place that in years.

With misgivings he approached his father's desk. This room was the least appealing one in the house for him. It was the place where his father had spent all his time questioning Grant's decisions. His friends, where he was going to school, his choice of career. In this space his father had tried to explain why he was divorcing his mother.

But none of those things he wanted Sara to know.

He told himself he had moved past those days but entering his father's ethereal personal space had brought them back in a flash. Grant looked at his father's leather desk chair. The last time he'd sat on that piece of furniture he'd been a kid, sitting on his father's knee. A week ago he wouldn't have even said that was a real memory. What had changed? Everything.

He took a deep breath and reached across the top of the desk for the business checkbook lying there.

Sara entered and waited close to the door.

"I'll have this for you in a sec." Grant picked up a pen and started writing.

"Great. You know, this is my favorite room in the entire house. Outside the kitchen it's the homiest, most comfortable."

Grant closed the checkbook with a slap. "It's not mine." He really was losing his mind. What had made him say that? He had no intention of having a conversation about how he felt about this space.

"Why? The room fits you. Right down to the desk."

Grant turned. He handed her the check then walked over to look at the bookshelf but at no book in particular. "This is where my father always called me on the carpet, so to speak."

"Ah, I can see why it might not be your favorite room, then."

"I was never good enough for him. My grades, girls I dated, the fact that I sided with my mother in the divorce, and the list goes on. Have you noticed that there are no pictures of me or my brother anywhere in this house? Particularly in here, his inner sanctum." The words sounded bitter even to his ears.

"I didn't know you had a brother."

"Exactly. In this house…" he waved at the structure "…we don't exist. He wiped us out of his life. Or at least let Evelyn do it." Shaking his head, he concluded, "It doesn't matter."

"I think it does." Sara came to stand beside him. Her hand rested on his arm for a second and was gone. That brief touch eased the tension in his shoulders a fraction. Trying to ignore that surprising effect, he almost missed her question.

"So where's your brother?"

"He lives in some commune out west. I see him about once a year."

"I always wanted a sibling." She moved away. "At least you still have your mother and him."

Grant missed her being close. He frowned. "Do you know why your mother left?"

Sara had her back to him. "No. My father was still at work when she decided to go. What she didn't know was that he had to work overtime that day. It was late when he got home." She fiddled with a statue of a golfer on the end table.

"So that's why you don't like staying by yourself." Inexplicably angry, he growled, "She shouldn't have done that."

"I know. Leaving was bad enough but to leave me alone was worse."

"Parents just have no idea sometimes what they are doing to their children."

She paused a moment then said, "Well, we're certainly a dysfunctional pair to be caring for a baby."

For some reason Grant didn't mind being classed with Sara. She made it all seem doable. "I would say we are. But Lily is going to have a better upbringing than I did."

Later that evening Leon called to ask Grant to join him for a golf game on Saturday. Grant had to turn him down because of his obligation to care for Lily.

"So, have you made up your mind about a wife?" Leon asked.

"No."

"This isn't something that you can drag your feet about. The sooner you look like a stable family man the better."

"What am I supposed to do? Run out and just ask some-one off the street to marry me?"

"Come on, Grant. I've never known you not to be able to find a woman when you wanted one."

"For heaven's sake, Leon. We're talking about me get-ting married here."

"I know. But we're also talk about winning Lily's cus-tody case. They go hand in hand."

Grant sighed. "I do have someone in mind."

He spent the next few hours going through some of his father's belongings and thinking about his conversation with Leon. He had to do something soon about securing a wife. He headed for the kitchen. Sara was there, prepar-ing bottles for the next day. She already looked like the woman of the house as she worked efficiently. In fact, he couldn't imagine a better one. Sara was great with Lily. Kept the house organized and running smoothly. Despite a couple of confrontational words between them, they got along rather well.

Maybe they could work out a deal…

CHAPTER FOUR

SARA TURNED TO find Grant watching her from the door. Was something wrong? When she'd left him in the study he'd been a bit gloomy but otherwise fine. Now there was an odd look on his face, as if he was debating whether or not to say something.

"Sara, could you come and sit down for a minute?" He moved toward the table.

Trepidation grew in her. What could be going on? She wiped her hands on a dish towel and joined him.

He looked at her intently and finally asked, "Do you have a place to move to tomorrow?"

Whoa, she hadn't expected that question. What had brought that on all of a sudden? She'd told him briefly about being evicted but he'd said nothing more until now. She hated this subject. It made her sound like she couldn't handle her life. Still, she needed to answer honestly. "No. We're going to a motel until I have a chance to find one."

"Do you have a boyfriend, a serious relationship or are you married?"

That question truly came out of nowhere. It was worse than being asked about the eviction. The man was making her dizzy with all the twists and turns in the conversation. He was getting far too personal. This discussion had taken a decidedly uncomfortable direction. Kim had assured her Grant was a good guy, but was he some closet pervert? She was the nanny, not his live-in good time. She narrowed her eyes at him. "What exactly does that have to do with anything?"

"I just don't want there to be any conflict with your time."

What was that supposed to mean? Was he implying she hadn't been giving Lily the best care possible? It didn't matter because she was leaving in a few days. But why the concern now?

She sat straighter, giving him a pointed look. "I can assure you Lily has had *my* undivided attention and will have it until I leave." Unlike what she'd seen from him. "And not that it's any of your business but, no, I don't have a love interest."

"That's what I wanted to talk to you about."

What was going on? She was missing something here. "My love life?"

"Yes. No. Sort of."

She pushed her chair back, preparing to stand.

He reached out a hand as if to stop her. "Please listen to me."

She settled again but kept her look focused on him. "Then get to the point because I'm not seeing it."

"Is there any reason you can't get married?" He leaned toward her as if her answer was supremely important to him.

She'd had just about enough of this integration. He was starting to scare her. Grant looked like a normal guy so why all the irrational questions? If she hadn't needed the final week of pay, she'd leave right now. "No. Why?"

As if he'd sensed her apprehension, he eased back in the chair and stated in a firm, calm voice, "My stepmother's family wants to take Lily away from me. My lawyer believes I need to be married if I have any hope of keeping Lily. I know this may sound nuts and is completely out of the blue, but would you consider marrying me?"

Sara's back went ramrod-straight. Her breath caught and her heart thudded. She lunged off the chair, almost butting into him as he stood also. "You have to be kidding! You are nuts. You couldn't even remember my name when we first met. We've only known each other a week. You must have some over-the-top ego that leads you to believe that because I saw you in your underwear and we shared two meals together, I'd want to marry you."

He blinked a couple of times. "No. You have the wrong idea. It would be a business agreement only. We would be married just in name. It would only be on paper. As soon as I have custody and can find a permanent nanny for Lily, we can go our separate ways. Easy. I would make it well worth your while. You're being evicted. In exchange for marrying me I would see to it that you have a place to live. I'll buy you a house of your choice."

Sara paused. A house? He'd buy her a house? No more worrying about bad rental apartments or looming evictions? She shook her head. No, it wasn't an option. "You are crazy," she said.

Still, the carrot he dangled in front of her was tempting. No more worrying about her father having a home, or her. No more moving. Also she had to admit she was proud of Grant for going to such lengths to keep Lily. He was truly committed to the child. She had to admire him for that. "We don't even know each other."

"No, but we don't have to. I'll go about my business and you can take care of Lily like you are doing now. We just have to make it through the court hearing."

"When will that be?"

The tension in him visibly eased, as if he knew he'd captured her interest. "I don't know. Maybe in a month."

That was a long time. Marriage, even on paper, was a commitment she wasn't sure she could make. That was one of the reasons she wasn't in a relationship. She could never get past the beginning stage. Her fear of doing something wrong and being left was too strong.

Could she handle being around Lily for that amount of time and not have it rip her heart out when she had to leave? Would the pain be worth the prize of a house? But how long and how many more moves would she and her father have to make before they could settle somewhere permanently if she didn't agree?

"I don't know." She'd been big hearted before and had carried Emily, and what had it gotten her? Heartache when she'd given her up. If she agreed to Grant's plan she was afraid she was in for more anguish on a much grander scale. Having a baby had been huge, but marriage? She was old-fashioned, still believing you should love someone before you married them.

"The court would see you as the perfect mother. I can already tell you're great with Lily. I think we can get along for a month or so." His gaze caught hers.

She moved away until the backs of her knees touched the chair. "This is risky. You need to think about it carefully. Don't you have someone else you could ask? I don't think I'm the person for the part."

"I know this is a radical idea but my lawyer assures me that it's the difference between me keeping Lily or not." His gaze found hers. "I wouldn't ask if I didn't think it was the only way."

Somehow it hurt to know he was only offering marriage to keep Lily. It would be so much easier to say yes if he cared about her. But how could he? They didn't even know each other. Why couldn't somebody want her for herself instead of what she could do for them?

"Committing to someone you don't know is a major step." Just as she should have thought through agreeing to being a surrogate mother. It was a life-altering event.

He spread his large hands. "If you agree, will it be any different for me?"

No, it wouldn't. And she and her father would have a place of their own. This was the chance to see him settled once and for all. Her opportunity to find her own happiness and not always be worrying about him and their finances. "I suppose you're right."

"Then you'll do it?"

The offer was tempting. Too much so. No, no, no. She couldn't go there again. Become involved so deeply in someone else's life. How could she not when she was thinking of marriage? But this was to help Lily and her father. She would make the sacrifice and deal with the fallout when the time came. She gave a reluctant nod.

His eyes sparkled. "Great. I'll arrange a moving van first thing in the morning for pick-up on Saturday. Tell your father not to worry about anything. He'll be moving in here for a while until you can find a house you like."

He had it all planned out, just like that. She hadn't moved past the idea that she'd agreed. "Thank you. I'm sure he'll appreciate it." Even to her own ears she didn't sound like she believed it.

Grant stepped away, then turned to face her. "I'm asking you to put your life on hold for a while for me. It's the least I can do. This is a huge place and we have the room."

"Dad can't make it up the stairs."

"I was thinking of letting him have the pool house. That way, he'd have his own space."

Stunned, she said, "Thank you. That would be wonderful."

"Then it's a deal." He stuck out his hand.

Sara looked at it for a few seconds then placed hers in his much larger one. He closed his around her fingers. She felt an odd sense of well-being, security. As if Grant would take care of her.

"A deal."

"Only thing is that we have to keep our agreement between us. No one else needs to know."

"How am I going to explain all of this to my father?"

Grant shrugged. "Tell him it was love at first sight. I'm sure you'll come up with something. I have to let my lawyer know it's all settled." He headed toward the hallway.

If a tornado had picked her up and whirled her around, she couldn't feel more out of control. What was she getting herself into?

Now she had to call and explain what was going on to her father. But what could she tell him that he would believe? She hated lying. The only thing she could hope for was that her father would be so excited about having a place to live that he'd overlook the fact that she was marrying a man she didn't know. If her father knew the truth he'd disapprove. She didn't think she could convince him it was love at first sight, but she would try.

Being careful what she revealed, she called her father and shared what she could. She finished with, "Dad, I'll be there to help pack on Saturday morning and the moving van will be there that afternoon."

"I'm shocked but happy for you, baby girl."

Sara agreed with the first part of his statement and just wished she felt the same way about the last.

* * *

Saturday morning Grant woke with a terror in his heart greater than the idea of getting married created. Sweat beaded on his face. He was going to have to look after Lily all day without help. What did he know about caring for a baby? Nothing.

Sara was in the kitchen, finishing feeding Lily, when he walked in.

"I'll let you take over now." Sara placed a used bottle in the sink.

Grant went stone still. *He had to start this minute?* His heart rate picked up. He'd rather be doing two surgeries at the same time than be left alone all day with a baby.

She turned from the sink and studied him. "Is there something wrong?"

"Wrong?" he croaked.

"You've gone pale."

Could he admit it? Did he really have a choice? "I don't think I can handle Lily on my own all day. Can we come with you?" He sounded pitiful even to his own ears.

"Uh?"

"I don't think it's healthy for her to be left in my hands all day. I don't know the first thing about taking care of a baby." He rushed to add, "We would stay out of the way. The movers should do all the work for you anyway. I'll feed and diaper Lily. I just need to know I have backup in case something goes wrong."

Was Grant kidding? The look on his face said he wasn't. Sara had never seen someone appear more alarmed. For a second she was afraid she might have to pick him up off the floor. If they left right away she could get done what she needed to do before the movers arrived. Would taking Grant and Lily along really be that big a deal? Yes, it would, but she felt sorry for him.

"I guess that'll be okay."

A smile spread across his face. "I'll get Lily and we'll meet you at the car. Why don't we take the SUV? That way we'll have plenty of room and you can haul anything you don't want the movers to touch back here."

Sara couldn't help but grin at his enthusiasm. It was better than the sickly look he'd had on his face minutes before. And worlds better than the displeasure on his face when he'd pointed out there were no pictures of him in the house. "I'm afraid it'll be a rather dull day for you."

"I think it'll be a better time for me and Lily than the one we'd have here without you."

"Well, all right." Still, he would have to learn to do it himself some time. She wouldn't always be around.

"Great. Tell me what I need to do to get Lily ready and we'll go."

It wouldn't be much of a day off if she had to give him orders the entire time. "You need to change her and get her dressed."

A perplexed look came over his features.

"Take her to the nursery and start undressing her. I'll be up when I'm finished here."

"Okay. But don't be long."

With an exasperated sigh Sara rinsed the bottle. She had her work cut out for her. Packing and seeing about Grant and Lily. By the time she made it to Lily's room, Grant had the baby's clothes off. They had been discarded and were in a pile on the floor. With a clean diaper in his hand, he was at least making an effort to put it on Lily. Maybe he'd be better at taking care of Lily than she was giving him credit for. At least he was trying. Giving him time to figure it out on his own, she went to the chest of drawers and pulled out an outfit.

"Done." Grant threw his hands up as if he had scored at a sporting event.

Sara walked to the bed and peered down at Lily. The diaper was cock-eyed and the tabs were backwards instead of facing the front but the diaper was on.

In an effort not to discourage Grant, Sara patted him on the back. "Good job."

A bolt of awareness shot through her. Touching him reminded her of the time she'd stuck her finger in an electrical socket as a child. His back was solid, muscular. Strong.

"Hand me her clothes." He was so focused on what he was doing he had no idea of the effect he'd had on her.

Relieved that was the case, Sara gave him the onesie she'd picked out. "For a man who didn't tell me her name a week ago and only started holding her recently, you're sure getting into this."

He turned to her. "Sometimes a man can be stupid."

"Hey, I'm not going to touch that statement with a ten-foot pole." And she knew well how quickly a person could become attached to a baby.

Grant gave her a sarcastic smile.

Half an hour later they were at the carport ready to get into the SUV. Grant said a harsh word under his breath.

"What's wrong?" Sara patted Lily on the back. She concealed a smile, knowing full well what the problem was.

"I have to move the car seat. I wish I'd never put it into the car. You need a mechanical engineering degree to put one in correctly."

Sara laughed out loud at his rant. "I tried to tell you." When was the last time she had truly laughed? It was nice. Freeing. "Lily and I will wait over here on the steps while you put your expensive education to work."

"Thanks a lot. The least you could do is offer to help."

She made a move as if to hand Lily to him. "Do you want me to?"

Grant squared his shoulders. "And strip me of my manhood? Strapping in a car seat is the twenty-first-century equivalent of bringing home the meat."

Laughing and still holding Lily, she made her way to the stoop to wait. Based on the first few meetings with Grant she wouldn't have thought he could be so much fun. It didn't take as long as she'd have imagined for him to get the seat in place. He did struggle some and said a few expletives that could burn a roof but the seat was finally secured.

"My hero," Sara murmured as she placed Lily in the seat.

He glanced at her. "I heard that."

They were headed down the drive when he asked, "Which way?"

"Toward Englewood."

He made a right. "So tell me about your dad," Grant said as he made the turn.

"Well, he likes to read, work crossword puzzles and loves sports. He worked at a machine shop until he was hurt."

"So what have you told him about us?"

Was there really an *us*? A marriage in name only didn't constitute an us. "Just that we are getting married. Thankfully I didn't have to explain much because he was so concerned about us having to move he didn't ask many questions, but he will. I did say it was love at first sight."

"And when he finds out the truth about the marriage?"

"He won't like it but he'll understand. He's my greatest supporter."

"That must have been a nice way to grow up." His voice took on a regretful note.

The need to comfort him was strong but she wasn't sure he would accept it. "It was. I'm sorry about what happened between you and your dad."

With a shrug of a shoulder he muttered, "I've learned to move on."

She was confident he hadn't. It was much too raw when he talked about his father. Maybe it was best to change the subject. "So tell me about Lily's mother. I saw her portrait over the mantel. She was beautiful and obviously much younger than your father."

"She was. By twenty-five years."

"Interesting. Where does a man meets someone so much younger than him?"

"When his son brings her home. Evelyn was *my* girl-friend."

"Oh." That was where the bitterness toward his father came from.

"Exactly." He made the word sound like a piece of tile breaking.

"No wonder you've had such a hard time warming to Lily." She paused then added, "And they left Lily to you?"

"Not exactly. They didn't have time to make out a new will. I got her because there was no one else to take her."

"So why're you going to such lengths to keep her? Marrying someone you don't know and buying a house? If the aunt and uncle are nice, maybe letting them adopt her would be best. You could always visit." The second she'd said the words she knew she was wrong. That hadn't worked out for her. She still missed Emily. She'd only been the surrogate mother, but that didn't matter. Would Grant feel the same regret she did if he gave up Lily?

"Lily belongs with me. I'm her brother, her family." His tone permitted no argument.

They lapsed into silence, broken only by her giving directions.

Grant had no idea why he'd told Sara about Evelyn. He hadn't confessed that humiliation to anyone. What power did this woman have over him that he said and did things so out of character? What made him think she was any different than Evelyn?

Sara indicated an apartment complex entrance and he pulled in. She pointed right to the parking lot in front of a building. He drove into a slot.

As Sara unbuckled her seat-belt, ready to step out of the car, she said, "I'll get Lily. You take out the stroller and grab the diaper bag."

"Hold on a minute."

Sara gave him a questioning look.

"I've been thinking that we might need to act like we're in love in front of your father. You know, the typical touching and kissing that he would expect from a couple who's so eager to get married." If it had been any other situation Grant would have laughed at the horrified look on Sara's face. "Come on, Sara. The idea can't be that bad."

"I guess you're right."

"Don't you think we should practice a little so that you don't act surprised in front of him when I kiss you?"

"You plan to do that?"

"I don't want him to guess this isn't anything but a love match."

She seemed to study his lips. He shifted in the seat

slightly. He was used to women begging for his kisses and she was acting as if it were a death sentence.

"I guess we could. We just don't need to get carried away."

"I'll promise not to if you don't." Grant leaned toward her and to her credit she didn't back away. Her lips were moist and inviting. Her hands remained in her lap. With great effort he kept the kiss a simple touch of the lips.

"Okay, we have a lot to do and need to get going." Sara was already in the process of opening the door.

Right. What he wanted to do was pull her back to him and give her a proper kiss. To his satisfaction he noticed the small tremor of her hands as she released Lily from her car seat. The chaste kiss had affected her after all.

Soon their little party was headed up the walk toward the building. Before they could get to the door a short, balding man hurried toward them from the direction of an adjacent building. He called out, "Ms. Marcum!" Sara's steps slowed as he came nearer.

"Is everything okay?" Grant asked, putting a supportive hand at her back.

"Yes, it's just the manager."

Grant stopped pushing the stroller and she placed Lily in it.

The man came up to them. "Ms. Marcum, you and your father will be out today?"

Grant was developing a dislike of the man already.

"Yes. That's why I'm here. The moving van will arrive this afternoon."

"Good. I expect you to leave the apartment in the same condition you found it in when you moved in."

"Look." Grant pushed the stroller forward, drawing the man's attention. "Why don't you just stay out of Ms.

Marcum and her father's way for the rest of the day?" He pulled out his wallet and handed the man some bills. "That should cover any *issues* you happen to invent—I mean, find. Now, if you'll excuse us, my fiancée and I have packing to do. Sara, why don't you push Lily?"

She did as he asked and started up the walk. Grant followed.

"I could have handled him myself," Sara hissed.

"I know, but I enjoyed putting that open-mouthed look on his face."

"Dr. Smythe, I think you might like being a tough guy."

He shrugged. "He's a jerk. Which one of these apartments is yours?"

"Right this way. There's Dad now."

A man using a walking stick was headed in their direction. He was tall, slim and had a head of thick brown hair neatly combed into place. From his carriage he looked like a no-nonsense type of person. Sara must have acquired her personality from him.

"Hi, little girl," her father called.

"Hey, Daddy." She picked up her pace, meeting him halfway with a hug.

Neither of his parents had ever given Grant that type of reception.

When father and daughter let go of each other, Sara's father turned his attention to Grant and Lily. "So, who do we have here?"

Grant moved up closer to Sara and extended his hand. "Nice to meet you, Mr. Marcum. Grant Smythe."

The man gave Grant a firm handshake and a steady look. "I'm Harold. You're the doc my little girl is planning to marry so suddenly?"

Grant wasn't particularly comfortable with lying to the man but he couldn't take a chance on the truth slipping out. Putting an arm around Sara's waist, he smiled at her. "I am."

Sara's eyes widened but she didn't flinch.

Harold continued to study them before he said, "Rather quick, isn't it?"

To her credit, Sara stepped closer to Grant and squeezed his arm. "That's what love at first sight is all about."

Her father grunted and gave Grant a pointed look. "I know this isn't a good day to discuss this uninterrupted but I expect to later." Her father's attention turned to Lily. "And this must be Lily." Harold smiled down at Lily, who cooed and kicked.

Grant was relieved that Harold had dropped the subject of the marriage for the time being. When he picked it up again Grant would be prepared. By Harold's tone of voice Sara had obviously told him a lot about Lily. How much had she said about him?

"She's a pretty thing. Any chance I can hold her? I've always wanted a granddaughter," Harold said.

Grant didn't miss Sara's wince. What had caused that?

"Let's go in, Dad. You need to get off that leg and I need to get started with the packing."

They walked toward a ground-level apartment. Sara pushed the door, already open, wider. Grant let her father enter first and then pushed Lily through in her stroller.

The apartment wasn't large but despite the packing boxes he could tell it had been orderly and well kept.

"Grant, have a seat." Harold indicated the sofa. Boxes were stacked here and there around the room.

The furniture looked comfortable but worn. Parking Lily beside it, Grant sat and Sara's father took a seat in a recliner nearby.

"Dad, I told you I'd take care of the packing when I got here."

"I know, baby girl, but I'm not an invalid. A nice couple was moving in down the way and they gave me their boxes."

"Okay, I'm going to take a couple to my room and put some things in them that I'm particular about." Sara headed down a short hallway. "Anything you missed that you'd like me to box up for you?"

"I have my personal stuff packed and marked. The other is to be stored."

"Can I help you?" Grant asked.

"I've got it for now." Sara looked from her father to Grant and back again with concern in her eyes before she left. She must be worried about Harold's reaction to their marriage.

"Grant, I appreciate you giving me a place to stay on such short notice."

"Not a problem," Grant assured Harold.

"So, you take in people all the time?" Harold didn't pull any punches.

Something told Grant that the older man saw more than he let on. "Sara told me about you having to move out. I have plenty of room. I take care of my family. She and you are that now."

Harold nodded his head sagely. This man wasn't being fooled.

"Sara says you're a surgeon."

Now, this was a subject Grant could warm to. "I am. I do liver transplants."

"Keep you away from the house at night?"

Grant resisted the urge to squirm. What was Harold getting at? "It can. Why?"

"Sara isn't a fan of staying by herself at night. She shouldn't be alone in that great big house she's been telling me about. Now I can keep her company."

"Daddy!" Sara's voice was high with reprimand as she came into the room with a box in her hands. "I've been just fine. Don't be giving Grant a hard time."

Why hadn't she said something about being afraid? After her story about her mother he knew she didn't like being alone, but he should have guessed that there was fear there. He wasn't surprised the lights were ablaze when he came home at night. Not once had she let on she was scared.

He met Sara's eyes. "I've not been home a few nights but I promise I'll try to do better."

Harold nodded. "How about me getting my hands on that cute little girl?"

Sara lifted Lily out of the stroller and placed her in Harold's arms. He smiled down at Lily and bounced her up and down before giving his daughter a hard look. "You make sure the next one of these you have you keep. I need all the grandchildren I can get."

Sara has a child?

A stricken look came over her face. She looked away. "Daddy, point out where the boxes are that you want to take to the house so I'll know which ones to tell the movers about."

"The ones in the hall."

Sara went to them and marked them with a large black pen. Over the next hour she worked while Grant assisted when she would let him.

Harold brought up the subject of sports and he and Grant had a heated back and forth about a new baseball player in town. At noon they all shared a simple meal Grant had ordered in.

Soon afterward the movers arrived. Grant directed them to the boxes Sara had marked. Not long afterwards he said, "I think we need to get out of here. We're just in the way."

"I have a few more things to see about in the kitchen. Why don't you change Lily and I'll tell Dad we're ready to go."

Grant wasn't excited about the prospect of the chore but he'd promised to do his part if she brought him along. With Lily in his arms, he went to the living room to fetch the diaper bag.

Not much later, Sara joined him with a bag in her hand. "Are you sure I don't need to stay here until the movers are done?"

"Positive. I spoke to the lead man and he knows what needs to be taken care of and where to bring the boxes you marked."

A mover squeezed past them, forcing Sara to step closer to him. Grant saw Harold just behind the man. Wrapping his arms around Sara, Grant kissed her on the forehead. He liked the feel of her body next to his. Too much. He was starting to enjoy this playacting. He was disappointed when she moved away.

"Dad, it's time to go," she called.

"I'm ready when you are, baby girl," he said from behind her.

Grant pushed the stroller toward the SUV, leaving Sara and her father to follow. They joined him at the vehicle. After they had Lily settled in the car seat, the stroller stowed and were in their seats, he took Sara's hand across the console and asked in a cheerful tone, "Home?"

"Yes." Sara's voice was a little high but she grasped his hand in return. It felt right.

To his amazement, after a long time he was starting to think of the house he'd grown up in as home. He glanced at Sara, then into the mirror at Lily and Harold in the seats behind him. If he hadn't known better, looking in from the outside, they were a family. That was something he'd never planned to have.

By the next afternoon Harold was settled in the pool house and Grant had helped Sara move her things to her room. They had all just finished a light lunch while Lily swung nearby.

"So what should we do this afternoon?" Grant asked.

Sara gave him a questioning look.

"What?"

"I just figured that you had somewhere to be. Golf course, ball game, country club."

Normally he would but for some reason he wasn't interested in that kind of thing today.

"Nope." He glanced at Harold, who was watching them closely. "I thought I'd spend the day with you guys."

Sara made a little choking sound but soon recovered. "Well, I was thinking what a beautiful day it is and how much I would enjoy a walk along Lake Michigan."

It had been forever since he'd spent any time near the lake, or outdoors at all for that matter. "Sounds good to me. Since you didn't really get a day off yesterday, I think you should get your choice of what we do."

She scoffed. "And I think any time you're around you're the one making the choices."

"Not this time." The grin she flashed him made his heart flutter.

He scooted the chair back. "I heard they redid Shoreline Park. We'll go there. How does that sound?"

"Wonderful."

An hour later he pulled into the crowded parking lot of the park. Sara had fallen asleep on the way over and woke when he stopped the car. Harold had chosen to stay behind, saying he'd prefer a nap.

Grant had never spent an afternoon at a park with a

newborn and a woman but found he was rather looking forward to it. That had happened more and more often in the last few weeks.

"We're here?" She blinked at him.

"We are. I'll get the stroller out, change Lily and we'll be ready to go." Grant opened the door and climbed out.

"I'll see to Lily."

Grant made a mental note to say thanks to Kim for sending Sara his way. By the time he had the stroller out, she was almost through changing Lily. She handed the tiny wrapped up bundle to him to strap in. He had Lily settled and watched as Sara checked and double-checked the contents of Lily's bag, making sure they had everything they might need. Was Sara this meticulous about everything? Kissing? Touching? Making love?

Those were thoughts he shouldn't be entertaining.

Sara didn't strike him as a woman who hopped into bed with just anyone. Or a person who moved on to the next guy. She was more the big-hearted, committed type of person. Her devotion to her father alone said she wouldn't be interested in a short-term affair.

Yet Grant didn't intend to have anything but a casual affair with a woman. He'd been hurt and he wasn't opening himself up for that again. No matter how nice Sara was, could he trust her? She might say all the right things then leave him just as Evelyn had. He wouldn't risk it.

Not now, not ever.

Sara looked out over the blue-green water of Lake Michigan. It rippled calmly against the shore. Although the sun was shining, there was a nip in the air. Couples were walking hand in hand along the paved path.

She'd held hands with Grant yesterday. It had been for her father's benefit but she'd still enjoyed it. Even though

Grant's actions had been playacting, a tingle had gone through her with each of his touches. She was going to have to get control of herself or she would be in more trouble than she'd imagined.

Families with their children on bikes zig-zagged their way past them. She waited for Grant. She turned to find him putting a second blanket over Lily before he locked the SUV. He'd come a long way from the first few days after she'd met him. She especially liked the change in him toward Lily. The man was starting to grow on her, even though she didn't like to admit it.

She was enjoying her day. Now that she better understood Grant, she could appreciate why he'd been so angry and had snapped at her when they'd first met. His family life hadn't been easy either. She felt sorry for him, which she was confident he wouldn't appreciate. On top of being horribly wounded by his father, now he was responsible for Lily. He must almost be at his tipping point.

Watching Grant push the stroller, she noticed he was a natural. He would make a good father to Lily. Would she have been a good auntie if she'd stayed in touch with Emily? She'd made her decision. Lifting her chin, she reminded herself that time in her life was behind her. Those thoughts should be buried and not brought up again. Unfortunately, being around Lily seemed to have resurrected them all. She had to keep her emotions in check or these two people would break her heart.

Sara refused to ruin a wonderful day by going there. She focused on Grant.

"What?" he asked. "Why're you looking at me that way?"

"I was just thinking that you're really picking up on this baby stuff."

He didn't meet her eyes as if he felt embarrassed. "I don't know about that. I still think there's a lot to learn."

"There's always more to know."

He shrugged. "Let's just say that Lily and I are figuring out how to get along."

"I'm glad. She deserves people around her who care. Every child does."

He didn't say anything for a few paces. "Your father implied you've had a child."

Sara didn't want to go into all of that with Grant yet if she didn't he'd probably keep pushing until he had an answer. She would make it short and to the point. "Some close friends wanted to have a baby but couldn't. I had it for them."

He stopped strolling. "You were a surrogate?"

"Yes. Now you know what my father meant by that comment yesterday."

"Really?" His voice held his obvious shock. "I had come up with a number of scenarios but that wasn't one of them."

"I don't imagine it would be."

"So what made you decide to make such a monumental choice?"

"You mean like marrying someone you hardly know so that he can win a custody case?"

Grant gave her a sheepish look. "I guess I deserved that. I really shouldn't be surprised."

She stared at the ground. "What does that mean?"

"Just that you have a big heart and you're a nurturer by nature. That was such a commitment."

There was that word. Sara had only been committed for nine months, then she'd run. Just as her mother had. Commitment wasn't in their blood. "You're right. So few people understand that." Including her. She shivered.

"Are you cold?" Grant asked. Before she could answer

he pulled the light blue cable-knit sweater he wore over his head and handed it to her. "You should be warmer with this."

She took the sweater. "But you'll be cold now."

"I'll be fine. My shirt has long sleeves." He checked on Lily.

Sara pulled the sweater on and adjusted it around her body. Grant's body heat surrounded her like a blanket of warmth. "It's a little big."

"Do you mind...?" Grant removed the collar of her shirt from inside the sweater and pulled it up around her neck. He brushed a lock of her hair back. "Perfect."

If she'd been cool before, she wasn't any longer. Both inside and out. Heat had flooded through her the second Grant had stepped close. She stuffed her hands into the pockets of her jeans to stop herself from reaching for him. If he really understood who she was, that she'd run first chance she got, he'd have nothing to do with her.

Grant's mouth came towards hers.

Sara's breath caught. Should she let him kiss her? More importantly, did she want him to?

His breath brushed her lips.

They tingled in anticipation. This wasn't for practice. For her father's sake. If she allowed it their relationship would change from one of business to something personal. Could she handle that? Would a kiss be worth the emotional upheaval? But what of the pleasure?

"Help, someone help!"

Grant's head jerked back. A woman came running toward them.

"See to Lily," he ordered Sara, as he rushed toward the frantic woman.

Reaching her moments later, he nodded as the woman

said between gasps, "There's been a bike accident. I saw it happen from here. Bad."

"I'm a doctor. Show me where. Then call 911."

She pointed on up the winding path. The injured people weren't visible. He glanced back to see Sara pushing Lily along the path at a bouncing pace. Grant took a more direct route over the grassy area.

A minute later a group of people gathered on the path came into view. As Grant approached he assessed the situation. There were two damaged bicycles lying on the ground, one just off the path and the other still on the cement. Taking a closer look, he could see two men were involved. Thankfully, both still wore their helmets. At least he wouldn't be dealing with bad head injuries.

Just as Grant arrived at the crowd another biker rode up and jumped off her bike.

"George, are you okay?" she was asking the man lying in the grass.

There was a groan from George, so Grant went down on one knee beside the other man, who had no one with him. The biker's arm was twisted into an unusual position beside him.

"I'm a doctor. What hurts?"

"My arm. I think it might be broken. Also the side of my face hurts." The man turned his head to show Grant. A couple of layers of skin were missing from temple to jaw.

"Lie still. An ambulance is on the way. I'm going to leave you to check the other guy. I'll be back to help you with that arm. Hang in there."

Grant moved to the other biker. "I'm Dr. Smythe. How're you feeling?"

"Mouth busted." Blood streamed out of the right side of it.

"His leg has a big gash. I'm his wife." The woman beside him pointed down at his leg.

Sara pulled up beside them with the stroller. Lily was crying, probably from her rather wild ride. "How can I help?"

"Just take care of Lily and watch for the ambulance." Sara was already picking the child up. "We need something to use as a compress on this cut," Grant said to no one in particular.

A baby diaper was thrusted into his face. He looked up to find Sara holding it.

"It's adsorbent and you can possibly attach it around the leg, using the Velcro." Sara handed Lily to the woman who had told them about the accident. Lily's cries were beginning to calm as the woman jiggled her.

Sara had already returned to going through Lily's diaper bag. "What kind of injuries does the other man have?"

"Broken arm. Face lacerations." Grant finished applying the diaper. "Hold this firmly. Like this." He showed the man's wife.

Sara was already moving toward their other patient. She dropped the bag on the ground beside the injured man and continued going through it as Grant joined her. "I've got a bottle of water, a clean burp pad." She looked further. "An extra blanket."

"Roll the blanket. We can fashion a sling out of it. Where's that ambulance?" Grant grumbled. To the biker he said, "Okay, we're going to sit you up. I'm going to support your arm. Sara here..." he looked at her for a second "...is going to put a sling around it. You're going to be fine. You may have to hold off on the biking for a few weeks but you'll be at it again soon."

Together he and Sara worked slowly and methodically to ease the man into a sitting position and get the arm immobilized. To Grant's relief, the sound of an ambulance siren filled the air.

Sara stood. "I'll direct them in." She was gone.

A few minutes later the ambulance pulled across the green to where they were. Grant explained to the emergency responders what had been done for both men. As the ambulance left, Sara, with Lily in her arms, came to stand beside him.

"You and Lily okay?" he asked.

"We're both fine."

"We'd better go. It's getting dark." Grant collected what contents of the bag remained, walked over to the stroller and brought it back to where Sara stood. She placed Lily in it and covered her. They started down the path in the direction from which they had come. "I appreciated your help. The diaper was quite brilliant."

"Thanks."

"You were an impressive emergency nurse."

She chuckled. "I've not done much of that since I was in school."

"I know what you mean. It's a completely different animal from a sterile OR. We made a good team."

She smiled. "We seem to be doing that rather often."

What kind of team would they have made during their almost kiss? Something told him that it would have been more explosive than their practice one. Even now a keen feeling of disappointment filled him. He still wanted to kiss Sara. If he did he would be breaking his agreement to keep their relationship strictly business. Surely one real one wouldn't matter? But would he be satisfied with that? He was afraid he might not be.

Did he dare take the chance?

CHAPTER FIVE

MONDAY AFTERNOON SARA was in Leon's office with Lily in her arms. After introductions Leon indicated a chair in front of his desk. "Sara, have a seat."

Grant remained standing near a large bookcase filled with legal volumes. He had a brooding look on his face. Wasn't he happy? After all, this was his idea.

Leon pushed some papers toward her. "You'll need to read these and sign them."

Lily whimpered.

"Let me have her." Grant stepped forward and gathered Lily into his arms. After their day together on Saturday he'd become much more adept at dealing with her.

Leon gave Grant an almost comical look. "Who are you?"

Grant glared back at him and started jiggling Lily. "Just see to Sara."

She read through the legal documents then looked at Grant. "This is too generous."

"No, it isn't. I need you to do this."

She'd seen that determined look before. He wouldn't be changing his mind. She signed where indicated and pushed the papers back to Leon.

"You both know that this can't look like a slipshod wedding," Leon said as he placed the papers in a folder. "It has to appear like the real thing. It doesn't have to be grand but it does have to be more than the justice of the peace."

Sara glanced at Grant. He had a rather sick expression on his face that matched how she felt.

"It'll need to take place soon because Lily's custody hearing is at the end of the month."

"Won't the judge be concerned that we have only been married a short time?"

"I'm counting on him not asking the length of the marriage. He'll be more concerned about there being a marriage and stable home."

She and Grant left Leon's office and were waiting for an elevator when Sara said, "I don't think I can handle a baby, look for a house and organize a wedding all at the same time."

Grant handed Lily back to her. "Don't worry about it. I know just the person to take care of everything."

That evening Sara answered her phone.

"This is Clarisse Smythe, Grant's mother. Is now a good time to talk?"

Panic stirred in Sara. What was Grant's mother doing, calling her? Probably to lambast her for marrying her son for money.

"Yes, it is. Lily is asleep."

"Lily. Brett's offspring." The words were as bitter as the wind blowing in Antarctica in the winter. "Why Grant wants… But that's not what I'm calling about. Grant says you two are getting married. He's asked me to take care of the wedding. What size are you?"

"Size?"

"You'll need a dress, won't you?"

"I guess so." Sara didn't sound too confident even to her own ears. "I'm a six."

"Do you have a preference?"

"I guess not. Something simple, I think."

"That's what Grant said as well. Shoe size?" The woman was demanding.

Sara told her. This conversation was growing more uncomfortable.

"Do you have anyone in mind for a maid of honor?"

"I hadn't thought about it. I guess I could ask Kim."

"Would you please contact her and ask her to call me? Here's my number." Grant's mother rattled off a phone number. "I'll see to her dress as well. Do you have a preference of color?"

"No."

"Good. That'll make it easier. That's all I needed. See you the week after next in North Carolina."

"North Carolina?"

"That's where the wedding will be held."

Not until that moment had it sunk in that she was truly getting married. To Grant.

Clarisse didn't seem to take a breath. "I look forward to meeting you. Grant says you're quite lovely."

Grant thought she was lovely? Sara stood there in wonder, looking at the red dot that indicated the call was over. When had her ordered and rather dull life spiraled out of control? Probably the minute she'd met Grant and he'd thrust Lily into her arms.

She dialed Kim's number. They talked about how the nanny job was working out. When there was a pause Sara asked, "Would you be my maid of honor?"

"You mean someday?"

"No, the weekend after next." Sara worked to make her tone sound even, not nervous.

"Who are you marrying?" Kim's voice rose. "You haven't been dating anyone that I know of."

"I'm marrying Grant."

"As in *Dr. Grant Smythe*?"

"Yes."

"Boy, girl, you work fast. Tell me how this happened. *I* would've taken the job if I had known that having the sexy Dr. Smythe was part of the deal."

Sara was already unsure about the decision and Kim wasn't helping. "Will you be my maid of honor or not?"

"Of course I will."

"Thank you. Grant's mother is handling all the arrangements. You need to call her and give her your dress size and she'll give you the particulars. Here's her number." Sara reeled off the number Clarisse had given her. "I hear Lily crying. I have to go."

Sara hated lying to her friend and to her father. If word slipped out about the background of their marriage, Grant's custody case might be damaged. She would just have to live with it and explain all later, hoping they would understand.

Despite being nervous about the wedding in general, Sara liked the routine that the household settled into. Grant said goodbye each morning to her and Lily before he left. He even took a moment to touch or hold Lily. It was as if he was starting to see the child less as his father and ex-girlfriend's insult to him and more as a charming new human worth getting to know. Sara hoped for Lily's sake he was thinking less of her as a sister and more as a daughter.

Most evenings he was at home in time for dinner. A few evenings he brought in takeout. On another he cooked. At breakfast she offered to cook a meal in appreciation for those he'd provided. He was very complimentary about her skills.

Her days revolved around Lily and despite her best efforts the little girl was working her way into her heart.

With each baby smile or new accomplishment Sara's heart warmed further. She did her best not to think of Lily as hers but fear started to bubble in her. It would be difficult to give her up. The same concern nagged at her regarding Grant.

No matter how she lectured herself, she couldn't seem to stop going down the slippery slope. She spent too much time thinking about him sleeping in the room down the hall, or looking forward to him coming home at night, or, worse, his touch. When her father was around Grant made sure they appeared like a couple in love, even to the point of giving her a kiss on the cheek or forehead. Each show of affection only made Sara wish for more. She tried to do her part but it didn't come off being near as effortless as Grant's was.

Her time with him and Lily was becoming more domestic with each day. Less employee and nanny. On one level it was nice, on another it made her nervous because she liked it too much. As the week wore on she looked forward to her day off, hoping she could regain some much-needed perspective and have a chance to clear her head. Grant and Lily were temporary in her life and she needed to keep that fact fixed firmly in her mind.

Sara was surprised to see Grant show up early on Friday evening still dressed in his scrubs. Usually he was wearing the same dress shirt and pants he'd left in earlier in the day.

"I thought you might not be home until late." Sara pulled Lily out of the swing and put her into the bouncer to feed her.

"Why's that?"

"You've been home every night this week and I just assumed you'd have something else to do on a weekend night."

"Are you tired of me?"

"No, that's not what I'm saying."

He smiled. "Good, because I kind of like coming home to someone at the end of the day."

With his relationship with his father on the rocks and his mother and brother living so far away, had he been lonely?

"We're glad to have you here. This house is too big for just Lily and me." And she meant it. She stepped to the counter to get Lily's bottle. "Your mother called again today."

"Does she have all the wedding arrangements made?" Grant took a seat at the table and played with Lily's foot.

"She wanted to know if I have a flower preference."

"Mind if I do that?" He indicated the bottle. "Do you?"

"No."

In regard to Lily he'd certainly turned over a new page. He made a few false starts but soon caught on to the process of feeding Lily. Watching a man take care of such a small human was a type of pleasure she'd not experienced before.

"I hate to say this but I think my father is waiting for you to have that discussion about marrying me. I know ours is a business arrangement but he doesn't. He's sort of old-fashioned about things like that."

Grant looked at her. "I should have already done that. I'll take care of it right away."

"Thanks. I know he would appreciate it. He's sort of been hinting." There would be questions later about their marriage but maybe his and Grant's discussion would ease the pain. It would at least look like Grant had asked for her hand in marriage, which would make her father happy. He'd had such a hard time when she'd agreed to be a surrogate mother that she could only imagine his reaction to her involvement in a trumped-up wedding.

She focused on Grant and Lily again. With the skills

Grant was exhibiting with Lily he could be nothing less than a caring and compassionate surgeon as well as father. When he was done he wore a self-satisfied grin.

"Would you like to bathe her?"

He looked uncertain but the terror that had once filled his eyes was missing. "Do you mind if I assist you? I don't think I'm ready to do it alone."

He needed to learn. One day she would be leaving, no matter how difficult it would be to do so. "You're welcome to help but it's nowhere near as difficult as transplant surgery."

"Maybe so, but I did train for that and I have zero experience in bathing a baby."

She smiled. "You're in luck. I did train in nursing school for it. Why don't you carry Lily up and undress her? I'll wash up her bottle and be there in a minute."

By the time she made it to Lily's room Grant had her completely undressed. He stood in the middle of the room, humming a current tune as he did a box step with Lily in his arms. It was the most uninhibited she'd seen Grant. Almost as if he'd let go of some of the animosity he'd been carrying. This was a side of him she was sure few had seen. Sara felt honored that she was one of those.

He looked at her. "Hey."

"Hi, there."

"You want to join us?"

A ripple of uncertainty went through her. She shook her head. "I don't think so."

He opened one arm wide and said, "Aw, come on. You never know. It might be fun."

Sara wanted to. What would it hurt if she did? Ignoring her fear, she stepped into his arm and he lightly wrapped it around her waist. One of her hands went to his forearm and the other rested on Lily's back. Could she ever have a true moment like this in her life? Her child. Her family.

Just a crazy dream. She couldn't get caught in the trap of thinking theirs would be a marriage in reality.

Together they shifted in a small circle.

Being this close to Grant was heady. His deep hum filled the room as he moved smoothly around the floor. He smelled slightly of Betadine, which was so much a part of his profession. She didn't find it offensive. It just reminded her that his business was to save lives.

She looked up to find Grant's rich coffee gaze on her. There was a question there. Desire. Her heart thumped hard but she managed a smile. His head lowered. Her breath caught. He hesitated as if waiting for her permission. Her lips parted. Grant's mouth moved closer. Time slowed. Lily cooed between them, her head resting on his shoulder. Sara silently begged for his kiss. He no longer moved his feet. Finally, blessedly, his lips found hers.

Grant's mouth was firm. Warm. She rose on her toes. His lips slid over hers, finding a more perfect fit. He pulled her tighter against him, pressing his mouth to hers. Melting, smooth heat rippled her. She'd been kissed before but not so that she shivered and burned at the same time. She opened for him.

It was all about desire, discovery, and acceptance.

Grant jerked away. "Ah, Lily."

There was a wet spot on his scrub shirt. He chuckled.

Sara's laugh held a nervous note. "I guess someone is trying to tell us it's time for a bath. Looks like you're going to need one too."

Need filled his eyes.

Was he thinking about something else? Sara forced herself back to reality. She took Lily. "I'll get her started while you take care of that shirt."

In the bathroom she picked up the plastic baby tub and placed it in the larger tub.

"So what do I need to do?" Grant asked from behind her. She glanced at him.

He'd removed his shirt and his shoes. With his chest bare he was the sexist sight she'd ever seen. Her pulse rate went into overdrive. If she didn't get control he would catch her staring. Grant was hitting all her emotional spots tonight. Did he have any idea of how his kiss had affected her? Her heart was still pounding too fast.

"You can get a washcloth and the bottle of baby soap from the counter." Sara turned the water on, letting it run until it was the correct temperature. Pushing the tub under the water, she filled it.

Grant said from behind her, "You're amazing to watch. The way you do all this one-handed."

"It comes from practice."

"I don't think I'll ever get the hang of it."

"Yes, you will. Why don't you take Lily and lay her in the tub? Remember to always check the temperature. More babies than you know get scalded."

"Yes, Nurse Marcum." He flapped his hand in the water.

She smirked and handed Lily to him. The back of her hand brushed his chest as she did so. She stepped away quickly. Lily's bath was becoming far too tantalizing. She was dreaming of things that could never be. Like Grant slowly running a bath cloth over her.

Grant went to his knees, gently placing Lily in the tub.

"Squirt a dab of soap on the rag and then just wash her. Start with her face and work down."

He went to work with the same passion he approached

everything. That he'd be the best and succeed. She could only image that same intensity extending to the bedroom. The thought only made her tingle in places better left alone.

While Grant moved the cloth over Lily, Sara enjoyed the play of his muscles across his shoulders. With each motion they flexed and released. The urge to touch, run her fingers over his skin was so great her hand was halfway there when he said over his shoulder, a grin on his face, "I'm done. What now?"

She was jolted from her daydream. *Did he have any idea what I was doing? Was about to do?*

"I'll get you a towel." Collecting herself, she pulled a hooded baby towel out from under the cabinet.

Grant was already standing with Lily in his arms when she turned around. Sara placed the cap over Lily's head and Grant worked the towel around her. He looked down into Lily's face with something that was not yet love, maybe infatuation. What a wonderful father he would be to Lily if he'd only let go of all the hurt. He would commit. Not run away. As she had done and would do.

"I'll lay out clothes and let you dress her. While you do that I'll straighten the bathroom."

Gone but a few minutes, she returned to find Grant had already dressed Lily. Sara smiled. Lily's onesie sleeper was on backwards but she said nothing. It wouldn't hurt Lily and it would damage Grant's new-found confidence if she criticized or corrected him. Something told her he'd had far too much of that in his life.

It was time to go. She didn't belong in this family scene. "I'll let you finish putting her to bed. I have some things to take care of in my room. Dad doesn't go to sleep until late. Good night."

"Sara, I thought—"

Did he think they would continue where their kiss had

left off? She would like to but that wasn't wise. Using her mind instead of her heart, Sara met his gaze. "You've got this. You'll both be fine."

She left off, *without me*.

Grant felt a small grip of panic when Sara and her father left Lily with him the next morning. His talk with her father had gone better than he'd expected. Sara's dad was concerned about how quickly the wedding had come about and that he didn't want his daughter hurt, but in the end he had seemed accepting. He loved Sara and only wanted the best for her. Grant had promised he had no intention of breaking her heart.

Between that discussion and the memory of his and Sara's kiss Grant hadn't slept much the night before. Their kiss had kept playing through his mind in vivid color. He wanted another one. A deeper, hotter, wet one. When she had left him with Lily he'd wanted to scream, *Come back*. Knowing she was sleeping next door hadn't eased the nagging want either.

Right now, he had a baby to see about. With Sara's help he'd gained confidence where Lily was concerned, but spending an entire day with an infant still brought dread and apprehension. Would he be as inadequate at caring for Lily as his father had said he was? How did the man manage to command so much power over him, even from the grave? He'd moved past those days, or at least he told himself he had. It didn't help that Sara had asked, "Are you sure about this?"

"We'll be fine. Go on. Enjoy your day."

She'd nodded and headed for the door. With one last look and a half-smile, Sara had pulled the door closed behind her.

More than once she'd proved she believed in his abilities

with Lily but still those old hurts came back when someone questioned his capabilities. The only area of his life
where he was completely comfortable was in his medical
skills. Those his father had never questioned because he'd
known nothing about that world. He wasn't here now to
question what Grant did, so why did his father's old words
still make him feel inadequate to the job of caring for Lily?

Everything in his life felt out of line. He wasn't sure
what was happening between him and his tiny sister, but
he really didn't understand what was going on between
him and Sara. He'd not planned to dance with Lily or in-
vite Sara to join them. He'd been surprised when he had
and she'd accepted. Been even more so when he'd kissed
her and she'd returned it.

The memory of Sara's uncertain then acquiescent hon-
eyed response would keep him humming all day. He already hungered for another kiss. Would she allow one?
Everything was spiraling out of his control. He needed
together time with Lily and Sara needed time away. He
wanted space to think about his growing feelings for both
his sister and Sara.

Somehow Lily was starting to feel less like his sister
and more like his daughter. Would his father have been
pleased? Maybe it was time to get past caring. He was responsible for Lily and he would do his best and that was
all anyone could expect.

Grant had had no real idea that one large flour-bag
size person could dominate his entire day. Sara couldn't
have made it down the drive before Lily started scream-
ing. Grant whisked her out of the swing and took her upstairs to change her diaper. Still she whined.

He bundled her into a blanket and went to the rocker.
Maybe all she needed to settle down was some motion.
Sitting, he started the chair moving. That went on for an-

other thirty minutes to no avail. Lily would quieten for a few minutes, just long enough for Grant to think she was asleep. The second he placed her in the bed she started again.

Surely he was capable of figuring out what was wrong. Old ingrained insecurities died hard. He refused to not meet the challenge. No way was he going to let his father's words damage his confidence regarding Lily.

Grant tried rocking her but it didn't help. In desperation, he gave her a warm bath. To his great relief, she sighed and slept. Taking the baby monitor from the stand, he tiptoed across the carpet and out the door. He worked long hours, but none had exhausted him like his failure to satisfy one child for a short amount of time.

In the kitchen, Grant poured himself a cup of fresh coffee and sat down to do some paperwork he'd been putting off. He had been at it for thirty minutes when he realized he'd left a file he needed in the car. Halfway across the kitchen to the door, he stopped and turned back for the monitor. He couldn't even retrieve an item from his car without thinking about Lily first. He sighed. This was what being a father was about.

Lily woke two hours later, before Grant could finish his work. He'd had no idea how much Lily would control his everyday life. In Lily's room, he picked her up and looked at her. She smiled.

He felt like he'd just been taken hostage. Would he ever get his heart back?

"Hey there, little girl." Little girl. Wasn't that what Harold called Sara? His daughter.

Was that what he was starting to see Lily as?

"Let's get you changed and go see if we can find some food."

Lily cooed. One more female working to wrap him

around her little finger. Where had his single-minded, focus on himself and his job gone?

With a minimum of fuss, he had Lily fed but the dishes were piled in the sink. Powdered formula was all over one counter and a section of the floor. His paperwork was spread out on the table, and Lily's seat still sat on the table. Whenever he'd tried to clean up, she had required his attention. Now she was changed and happily lying on a blanket on the floor beside him in his father's study.

The place was slowly becoming a place that Grant could tolerate. He was making it his own. The command his father had held over him was gradually ebbing away. Those days and ugly words would forever be with him but he now sat in his father's chair and held the authority. Grant looked at Lily. He would prove himself worthy. "I promise you'll always feel loved and supported."

Why couldn't his father have done that for him? What had happened to make his father be so hard on him? It was as if he'd expected perfection but only by his standards. Grant hadn't been able to give him that. What had driven his father? Grant had never questioned before that something might have been behind his father's expectations. He would have to give that some thought.

Sara called in the middle of the day to check on them.

"We're doing just fine." He spoke in a low voice.

"Why're you whispering? Is something wrong?"

She didn't think he could handle this. No, it was concern, not criticism. Sara would have never left Lily if she hadn't thought he would take good care of her. "We're just fine. Don't worry about us."

"Okay." She didn't sound convinced. "Do you want me to bring dinner?"

Dinner. He hadn't thought about eating lunch, much less dinner. "Sure." It sounded almost too casual to his own ears. He was afraid that if she didn't buy takeout he wouldn't get a meal. He certainly wasn't going to prepare one himself. "Get whatever you want."

"All right. Dad and I will see you in a few hours."

From what he could tell, he owed Sara thousands of dollars for what she did each day.

For some reason Lily was fretful again that afternoon. Grant went through every maneuver he could think of to make her happy. He did what he had done that morning, along with pacing the foyer floor and jiggling her.

"Hush, sweetie," he murmured as he held her close to his chest.

Nothing seemed to help. It hurt him to hear her cries of misery. Exhausted, he finally sat on the living-room couch, stretched out his legs, leaned his head back on the cushions, placed Lily belly to belly with him and rubbed her back. She made one last whimper and went to sleep. He joined her.

They were still in that position when Sara came home.

"So how did it go?" she asked with a grin as she looked down at them with a knowing gleam in her eyes.

"You can get an idea of how it went by looking at us. She was unhappy after eating, for some reason."

"She may just have a little bit of a bellyache."

He moved to sit straighter. "It didn't seem like a little bit when she was fussing for an hour."

Sara shrugged. "Sometimes that happens."

"You have her all the time. By the way, I applaud you for what you do." Grant caressed Lily's back.

Sara chuckled. "Babies can be overwhelming."

"That they can be." He gathered the still sleeping Lily into his arms and placed a kiss on the top of her head. "But I still enjoyed the me-and-her time. So how did the house-hunting go?"

"Pretty well. We found one that Dad and I both like."

"When you decide on one, let me know and I'll have Leon take care of the purchase."

"Thanks for talking to Dad. He seemed to be okay with us getting married so soon. You really sold him on the idea of love at first sight. I still don't like lying to him, though."

"He's a smart man. He'll understand."

"I think you've done enough nannying for the day so why don't you let me have Lily and I'll put her to bed?" Sara reached down to take her.

Grant caught her hand and caressed the inside of her wrist. "We missed you today."

She frowned down at their clasped hands. "Grant, we shouldn't—"

His cell rang. She took Lily then he dug into his pocket for his phone.

"Smythe. Yes. Yes. I'm on my way." He stood.

"I know. You're needed at the hospital." She made it a statement instead of a question.

"Yes. A liver has become available for a patient who has been waiting too long. I won't be home tonight. May even be gone most of tomorrow."

"I understand. I'll see to Lily."

And he could trust that she would. "Why don't you ask your father to sleep in the small room off the kitchen so you don't have to be in the house by yourself?"

She shook her head. "I'll be fine. I'm getting better about knowing the sounds of the house."

He caressed her cheek. "I don't want you to be scared when I'm gone."

"I won't be as long as I know when you're coming and going. Thanks for caring."

A few minutes later as he backed out of the carport he noted the light was already on beside the kitchen door. It would be shining when he returned. To his amazement he liked the idea that Sara would be waiting on him. They were already acting like a married couple. Why didn't that idea bother him more?

Grant had been gone over thirty-six hours. All he wanted was to get some much-needed sleep. He wasn't going to take the chance of waking Sara to let her know that he was home. She would just have to find that out on her own.

He stripped and climbed into bed, hoping to get a few hours of sleep before returning to the hospital. The alarm went off what seemed like only seconds later. He climbed out of bed, found fresh underwear and headed for the bathroom. He opened the door and blinked.

Sara stood there wrapped in a towel, combing her wet hair.

"What're you doing?" Her high-pitched words nearly hurt his ears.

"Sorry. I didn't hear the shower running."

Her eyes didn't leave him. "Why're you using my bathroom?"

"It's mine too."

"I thought you were staying in the master."

That idea made his skin crawl.

Her gazed went south and her eyes widened. She said calmly, "Grant, you don't have anything on. We talked about that."

"I don't usually wear clothes when I shower. You want to join me?" He tried for his most wicked look.

"I don't think that would be a good idea."

"You start off everything between us with 'I don't think.' Maybe you need to think less and enjoy more."

She shook her head. "I'm done here so you're welcome to the bath." Sara disappeared through the other door.

He watched her go with disappointment. What he really wanted to do was jerk that towel off and pull her into his arms. Being married to Sara was going to be interesting, and physically demanding.

Boxers still in hand, Grant turned on the water. He had to admit this was the most fun he'd had with a woman in a long time. Seeing Sara flustered, turning the prettiest shade of pink he'd ever seen when her gaze had been fixed on his morning erection, delighted him. She'd not shied away from looking.

After her surprise that they'd been sharing a bathroom for weeks, what would be her reaction when she learned that she'd been sleeping in his childhood bedroom all this time?

A couple of evenings later Sara was upstairs, putting Lily to sleep, when car lights shone through the window and the vehicle pulled into the carport. Grant had had another long day. The faint sound of the outside door opening and closing rose to the second floor.

Was he coming home every night because she was there? Her vanity wanted to say yes. But she knew better. It was more likely him making every effort to convince himself that he could do the job of being a good surgeon and parent to Lily. With a little help he was succeeding. She'd been very impressed with his efforts on Saturday. Both he and Lily had survived. And, from what she could tell, had bonded.

Her father had settled on the house they had liked. It was in a small neighborhood between Highland Park and Chicago. It had everything they would need close by. There was a senior citizen building, a park, shopping and easy access to the train into downtown. Maybe Grant was being far too generous but it was nice to know her father would be safe and secure from eviction ever again. Her father planned to move in right away.

It took Sara another thirty minutes to get Lily down for the night and her clothes laid out for the next day. Grant still hadn't stuck his head into the room to say he was home or check on Lily. He'd been vigilant about both over the last week. Why hadn't he tonight? Because of her reaction to him in the bathroom? Was he afraid that she might jump him and demand to have his body? The thought had occurred to her. He'd looked breathtakingly gorgeous in all his glory. She could only imagine the pleasure of having all of that as her own. But thinking that way was going to get her nowhere.

Going into the kitchen, she didn't find Grant there. She looked out the window to the pool and didn't see anyone there either. Was he still in the car? Opening the door, she searched the carport area and saw no lights.

She was starting to worry. Something was wrong. Maybe it wasn't Grant but someone else who had driven up. She shook the thought away and checked other areas of the house. Saving his father's den to search last because of how Grant felt about the place, she expected the lights would be off and they were. She moved to leave the doorway.

"Are you looking for me?"

She stopped short at the harshness in Grant's voice. He'd not used that tone since the day they'd met. "Why're you sitting in the dark?" She went to the nearest lamp and reached to turn it on.

"Leave it."

She stopped in mid-motion. "Why?"

"Just leave it."

"What's going on, Grant? What's wrong? Has something happen regarding Lily?"

"No."

She walked closer. Her eyes adjusted to the absence of light and she could see him sitting in the chair behind the desk. She came to stand at the corner nearest him.

Grant rubbed his hands over the worn brown leather of the chair arms. He rocked back. "Do you know that up until last week I've not been on my father's side of this desk since I was maybe seven?"

Sara didn't say anything. It wasn't a question she was expected to answer. He was off somewhere that didn't include her.

"He never allowed me to sit in his chair. Said I had to earn the privilege." Grant didn't say anything for a few moments. "I was never good enough."

"What has happened?" She all but whispered the words.

"Nothing, except I let a patient die."

"I'm sorry." Her hand went to rest on his forearm stretched along the arm of the chair. "I don't believe you just let a patient die."

He pulled away. "How would you know?"

Sara let her hand drop to her side. "Because I know the type of person you are. That you're the kind of doctor who cares deeply about your patients and others."

"So now you know all about me?"

"I don't. But I know how you treat me. Lily. I've watched you with my father. You care. You'd never intentionally let a patient die. I would swear you put all your knowledge and compassion into everything you do. Sometimes things happen that we can't control." Like your mother leaving for no reason. Or caring more about a baby that belonged to someone else than you should.

"He sat right here and said I'd never be a good doctor."

Anger roiled in her. If she could only tell his father off. "But you are. You know you are."

"Just what makes me think I'll be a good father to Lily? How do I have the audacity to think I would be good enough to raise a child? Or not be like him?"

"Forget about your father. Grant, tell me what happened today." She wanted to help him but she couldn't figure out how.

"The surgery was going fine and then it wasn't. It was as if the patient had an immediate negative reaction to the donated liver. I had promised the family that their mother would be fine. To trust me. But I let them down."

"You did the best you could. You can't control everything."

He jerked straight and glared at her. Speaking through clenched teeth, he said, "In my OR I do!"

Sara flinched as if slapped but didn't step away. "I don't need to stand here and tell you how many people you have saved with your talent. Or how important it is. There's a baby asleep upstairs who would have no home or someone who cared about her if it wasn't for you. My father and I have a roof over our heads because of you. Your father was wrong, so wrong about you. But you're the only one who doesn't believe that."

She turned to go. Grant grabbed her around the waist and pulled her into his lap. He buried his face in the curve of her neck.

Grant felt the instant Sara relaxed. She wrapped an arm around his shoulders as he pulled her tighter against him. He'd found his lifeline. From her had come all the right words, the correct indignant tone when scolding, but it hadn't been until she embraced him that his heart opened and accepted what she'd been saying. He held her, not moving for a long time. One of her hands went to his hair and smoothed it, as if he were a child looking for reassurance. For a moment he had been. What he had missed in this room had been someone to have faith in him, and he had that now. Sara had given him a gift. She believed in him.

He inhaled the richness that was her, a floral scent yet something wispy and sweet that was only Sara. Even her name calmed him. He nuzzled his nose against her skin before his lips touched it. Her hand stilled in his hair for a second then continued to caress.

She felt so good, so right in his arms. Her curves molded to his perfectly.

Grant released his hold on her marginally but she made no attempt to leave. He placed a kiss behind her ear. "Sweet, sweet Sara," he whispered.

Her heart thudded sharp and strong against his chest. She wasn't as unaffected by him as she led him to believe.

His lips brushed along her neck and then across her jaw. She turned toward him slightly and his mouth claimed hers. Heat fired in his gut and his manhood came to complete attention. His mouth moved across her lips, tasting and testing until her fingers found the back of his neck and nudged him closer. Sara returned his kiss with all the fervor he'd ever dreamt of. She shifted, turning in his lap and giving him better access.

Pleasure-filled moments went by before he pulled back. "I want you. Right now. Right here."

Sara blinked as if she'd forgotten where she was. Slowly she began to untangle herself from him. Grant tightened his grip. She looked him straight in the eye. "Grant, I won't be the instrument you use to purge all the memories this room has for you. When I make love with a man I expect him to be sharing it with me, not erasing ugly thoughts."

His arms slackened their hold. For once in his life he was truly ashamed. He let his arms rest on the chair arms, giving her an opening. "It's not that way, you know."

Sara rubbed across his shaft as she stood. He stifled a groan.

"You think about it. Despite how enjoyable being with you might be, doing so in your father's chair, on his desk or on the floor wouldn't be about you and me. It'd be about you and him." She walked halfway to the door and turned back. "I'm sorry about your patient. I know you did your best. You're a good man and a great surgeon, Grant. You're the only one who doesn't believe that."

He watched Sara go with pain in his heart and his groin. No one liked it when someone saw through them.

CHAPTER SIX

SARA WALKED AWAY from Grant with wobbly knees. She'd been kissed before. Heavens, it had been years since she'd been a virgin, but Grant's kisses had been the hottest, most all-consuming and addictive ones she'd ever experienced. She never wanted him to know what amount of self-control it had taken her to walk away.

She would have gladly swiped everything off his father's desk, sat on it and opened wide in invitation, but she wouldn't let Grant regret their being together by doing so. He was so honorable his guilt would eat him up because he had taken her that way.

With effort she made it to her room, showered and was in bed when sounds of Grant coming down the hallway reached her ears. He didn't stay long before he left again.

Where was he going?

The way he felt tonight and with what had just happened between them she'd best not search him out. She stayed awake late into the night, listening for his return and reliving those moments in the den.

Lily's cry jarred her awake the next morning. It wasn't until she was carrying her down for breakfast and they passed the living room that Sara learned where Grant had spent the night. Folded neatly on the end of one of the sofas was a blanket with a pillow on top.

Why hadn't he slept in his bed? A heady feeling filled her. Was it because he would have been too close to her? That was something interesting to contemplate.

On the kitchen counter she found a note: "I'm gone."

She smiled. Looking at Lily happily going back and forth in the swing, she could easily get used to being in Grant and Lily's world.

He was later than usual again that night but that was all right with Sara because she had time to get Lily down for the night. She was in the kitchen when he came in. He looked tired but his mouth lifted into a slight smile when he saw her. Her insides warmed each time she saw him. Would he say something about what had happened last night?

"Hi."

"Hey. You look like you could be hungry. Would you like me to fix you something to eat?" she offered.

"Come to think of it, I did miss lunch. But I'll get a bowl of ice cream or something. You're not the maid."

The man did like his ice cream. She'd started adding a carton to the grocery list each week. "I don't mind. Really. How about a nice omelet and toast?"

"Sounds wonderful. I'm going to wash up and be right back down." He was out the door before she could mention she wanted to talk to him. She would do that after he ate.

Sara was just finishing the eggs when he returned. "Have a seat. Food's coming up."

He pulled a chair out from the table, sat, and stretched out his long legs, crossing his ankles before leaning back with his arms crossed on his chest. His gaze remained on her as she worked. A zing of awareness went through her.

Conscious of his attention as she brought his meal to him, her heart beat faster. He pulled his legs in and sat straighter when she reached him. He was a handsome man but, more importantly, she liked him. Grant was a man who had taken his baby sister in, a man who suffered for a patient and a man who could laugh at himself. He was someone she could enjoy being around for a long time. That was not a place she needed to go.

"Thank you. This is a nice treat."

"Not a problem. Do you mind if I sit with you while you eat?"

"Of course not."

Sara took a chair catty-corner to his. She watched as he forked food into his mouth and chewed then swallowed. That mouth had kissed her the night before. She resettled herself in the chair.

"Okay, Sara, what's going on? I know it isn't about Lily because you would have already told me."

"I'm nervous about this wedding business. Are you sure you want to go through with it? It would take me awhile but I would pay you back. I would honor our business agreement."

Sara's statement hurt. They did have an arrangement but some part of Grant wished it could be more. Less matter-of-fact. It was like she'd turned off any emotion. She acted as if they were strangers who had never shared a kiss that had seared him to the soul. No matter how she argued they were strangers, he knew better.

"I can't stand lying to all the people closest to us."

He put a hand over hers, which rested on the table. Thankfully she didn't pull away. "We'll make it up to all of them after I have custody. I promise. I'll make sure that your father understands that I insisted it be this way."

Sara looked overwhelmed.

"Mother will have everything handled. The movers will see to your father. Hang in there with me."

She nodded and removed her hand from under his, then stood. "Get some rest, Grant. I worry about you working so hard. Good night."

Sara worried about him? When was the last time anyone had done that?

An hour later he was finishing up some work in his father's office. Really, it was his now. The thought didn't bring the pain he expected. It was slowly ebbing away. In its place was the dull throb of disappointment that he'd never have the chance for that true father/son relationship. What he would have to do now was build a solid father/daughter one with Lily. Based on the example he'd seen, could he? He would try. At least he knew what not to do.

As for he and Sara, he had no idea. She fenced herself away any time he came too close. If he created an entrance and stepped in, would she expect more than he was willing to give? Their kisses, which had been far too short for him, had confirmed in firework brilliance that there could be something exciting between them. When she'd stepped into his arms and he'd brought her close, the thought that this was how it should be had crossed his mind. Sara belonged with him and Lily. At least for the time being. They needed her. In more ways than one.

His work completed, Grant wandered through to the kitchen. Pulling out the ice cream, he scooped some into a bowl. Returning the container to the freezer, he took his bowl to the table.

A movement in the pool caught his attention. Sara was swimming, doing long lazy laps from one end to the other. The night was still cool but the pool was heated and steam rose around her. It gave her a mystical appeal.

He watched her as he ate. It wasn't safe to swim by yourself so it was his duty to be her lifeguard. At least, that was the excuse he gave himself. After all, hadn't he caught her looking at him when he'd been bathing Lily? It was only fair.

Finishing his ice cream, he placed the bowl in the sink. He couldn't help but walk to the pool. Sara was just coming up the steps out of the water when he stepped on the swim deck.

She jerked to attention. "Ooh. You scared me."

Just as lovely as ever. She wore a simple one-piece swimsuit that defined her curves to their best advantage.

"I didn't mean to." Grant couldn't help but stare. If he didn't know better he'd say he was starting to act like a lovesick puppy. "I came to the kitchen to get some ice cream and saw movement out here." He'd never admit to watching her for as long as he had.

"I couldn't sleep. I thought I'd try out the pool. I hope you don't mind."

"Of course not. You're welcome to anything here." *Including me.*

Picking up a towel from the chair, she wrapped it around herself. Disappointment filled him at the loss of the view. Why, of all the women he'd known, did this one unassuming female fascinate him so?

Sara sat in the chair then picked up a cup with a tea-bag tag hanging over the edge and took a sip. Her small sound of pleasure filled the air.

"Do you mind if I join you?" For a second he feared she wouldn't agree.

"Why not?"

It wasn't the warmest reception he'd ever received but he would take it. Settling on the lounge next to her, he stretched out. It was nice. He didn't take time in his life to just sit and be. Grant said nothing, knowing he'd already encroached on her time, but he couldn't bring himself to go back inside. She shifted to get more comfortable and took another drink from her cup.

The croak of a frog and the buzz of a bug joined the other night sounds. They were too close to the city to see the stars as he would have liked.

"I'm sorry your father is putting you through all this. I know you have some harsh feelings toward him."

"It may not have seemed that way last night but those have eased some since I've become responsible for Lily. Maybe it's that they're gone or that I have to think of someone other than myself. Or that I no longer have the time or energy to be mad."

A few seconds went by before she said, "I admire you. It's hard to change, especially from a direction you were going with such determination, only to reverse and go back the other way."

He liked her thinking. "I'm not sure I've earned admiration."

"You underestimate yourself. Look what you're doing for Lily."

Laughing self-consciously, he protested, "Don't make me into a hero. I'm afraid I would disappoint you."

"I don't know about that. You have a tough road ahead of you."

"I realize that. I'll have to make major changes in my life. Do you think I shouldn't fight for Lily?" He waited impatiently for her response. Why it mattered so much what she thought was a mystery to him.

"Oh, of course you should. I'm just saying it won't be easy. Ask my father."

"I'm sure it won't but I'll do what I have to do. Are you wondering why I think I should raise Lily?"

"No. It's enough that you want her badly enough to fight for her. You're more interested in her welfare than your feelings toward her parents. That's what being a good parent is about."

"Thank you for that. You're a tender-hearted woman, Sara Marcum." He'd said it with a note of reverence. In his experience, there were few he could say that about.

Sara had liked being complimented by Grant. Yet something about him said his respect wasn't given freely. She wasn't sure she deserved it either. She'd given up Emily. But she had never been hers to keep. Emily belonged to her friends. She had from the beginning. What Sara could carry the blame for was letting herself care too much. Allowing herself to think of Emily as hers. That wasn't going to happen with Lily. She couldn't think of Grant as hers either.

Unclear what had brought him down to the pool, she was still glad to listen. Apparently he needed to talk. He was confiding in her about his concerns. With each day they seemed to get more wrapped up in each other's lives.

Even if she desired that relationship all the time, she couldn't have it. Couldn't take the chance of hurting him and Lily when she left. She knew the agony of being left behind all too well. Once again she would know pain but it didn't matter. The decision had been made. At least her father would have a roof over his head for her sorrow. Practical things were what she needed to concern herself with, not matters of the heart. She would get over that, eventually.

"Thank you for helping me. It's mighty supportive of you," Grant said.

She liked hearing his voice on the night air. "I'm not sure being supportive is my most useful trait. Sometimes it gets me into trouble. Like getting married for a house." She grinned. "What do you consider your best trait?"

"I don't know. I'm known for putting my mind to something and making it happen. Maybe that's the reason that I've never understood why I couldn't please my father."

A shiver went through her that had nothing to do with the weather. What if he put his mind to having her in his bed? Could she resist him? Did she want to? It was time for her to go in. "I'm getting cold so I'm going to say goodnight again. See you in the morning."

Grant stood when she did, capturing her hand as she passed him. She looked into his angular face, made more intriguing by the shadows.

"Thanks for helping me out with Lily too. We both need you."

"We're helping each other out." Her fingers slowly slipped from his hand as she walked away. For once in her life she felt as if she had left something important undone.

A few days later it was moving day for her father. He and Sara were at the new house early to meet the truck. Over the course of the morning she opened and set up the kitchen as the movers brought in the boxes. Her father spent his time helping direct the men to where the furniture should be placed.

Sara was sitting on the floor, putting cookie sheets in order, when Grant came in the back door with Lily in his arms. He looked like a family man, nothing like the self-centered transplant surgeon she'd grumbled about the first day they'd met.

He held up a couple of paper sacks from a local hamburger place. "I bought lunch. Drinks are out in the car. You take Lil and I'll get them."

Sara smiled. Grant had taken to calling Lily by a nickname after the day they had spent together. It was nice to see how he'd warmed up to her. The relationship seemed less about what he had to do and more about what he wanted to do. He'd fallen in love with the little girl. Sara could understand how that could happen.

Grant placed the sacks on the table and slipped Lily into Sara's arms. He headed out the door again.

"Hey, Dad. Food's here," she called.

A few minutes later her father joined her. He sat in one of the kitchen chairs. "Let me see that little girl."

Sara passed Lily to him and started removing burgers from the bags and still Grant hadn't returned. "I'm going to see if Grant needs some help."

Going to the open front door, she watched him walking from the street through the yard, balancing drink cups in his hand. The moving van was still parked in the drive.

He was almost to the steps of the porch when one of the movers hollered, "Hold it, Jake."

Sara looked just in time to see a chest of drawers tip forward. One of men pushed the chest the other way, causing the dolly wheel to go over the edge of the ramp. The mover lost control and the cabinet came down, pinning the lower half of his body under the chest.

Sara squealed and rushed down the steps. Having already dropped the drinks, Grant ran to the man.

"Let's get this off him." Jake's voice was filled with panic.

"I'm a doctor," Grant said in a calm voice. "We have to do it slowly so that we don't cause further injury."

Sara came up beside him. Grant dug into his pocket and handed her his phone. "Call 911."

She did as she was told, giving the dispatcher all the particulars. While she talked, Grant and the other mover worked to unstrap the chest from the dolly and raise it off the injured man. By that time her father, carrying Lily, had come looking for them. Sara handed the phone to him. "911 is still on the line. Go down by the street and make sure they know where to come. I need to help Grant."

She didn't give her father time to say anything before she bounded into the house and grabbed some blankets she'd left lying on a bed and her nursing bag. Back outside, she put the blankets down near the injured man as Grant and Jake removed the dolly from on top of him. As soon as it was clear she covered the man with a blanket.

"I have my nursing bag."

"Good girl. We need to be prepared for shock." He checked the man's pupils. "What's his name?"

"Rick," Jake said.

"Rick, I want you to lie still. You may have internal injuries and we don't want to make them worse."

Sara handed Grant her stethoscope across the man's chest. He took it without question. Then she searched the bag. "I'll get his blood pressure." She put the cuff on Rick's arm and pumped it up. After Grant had listened to his heart he handed the stethoscope back to her. She placed it in the crook of Rick's arm and located a pulse. It was slow. She looked up at Grant. "His blood pressure is low."

Grant said to Rick, "I need to check your midsection. Let me know if it hurts." He moved the blanket back and started palpating the patient's stomach area. The man yelped when Grant touched his left side.

"His spleen?" Sara asked, from where she'd moved to his side.

"Good diagnosis. Check his pressure again. We don't need him to code on us before the wagon gets here."

Sara went to work again.

"I'm going to see if anything is broken this time." Grant slowly worked his hands up Rick's right leg. The man had no reaction. When Grant started touching his left leg near his ankle Rick hollered. "Okay. It looks like this leg will need to be immobilized."

Sara leaned over and pulled a blanket toward her. "Blood pressure's still going down. I'll roll this blanket up to use for support for the leg."

Grant reached over the man's head and snagged the other blanket and followed her actions.

The distant sound of the ambulance siren filled Sara with relief. The man's blood pressure was dangerously low. He needed to get to a hospital OR to have his spleen removed.

Grant checked Rick's eyes again. He glanced at her, his lips a tight line.

"Am I going to be all right?" Rick asked.

Grant placed his hand on the man's forearm. "You're going to be fine. A little patching up and you'll be out moving someone again."

The man gave Grant a weak smile.

The ambulance pulled to the curb and much of what happened after that was a blur. Sara took Lily from her father when she started to cry. Grant reported his findings to the ER doctor over the phone. The EMTs soon had the injured man on the gurney.

Grant joined her where she stood watching the ambulance drive away.

"How do you think he's going to do?"

"He should be fine if he has no complications. I'll check on him in a few hours. You know, I'd take you as a nurse in any emergency. You were great once again."

Sara couldn't help but glow at the compliment. "You weren't bad yourself. You know, I've had more emergencies in my life since I've known you than ever before."

"I'm glad I can add excitement to your life."

He did that. How exciting would it be, being married to Grant? Very, Sara suspected.

Grant wasn't sure how the next week or so was going to pan out but he was confident they wouldn't be easy emotionally.

The week after moving Sara's father he'd seen little of Sara and Lily, having been too busy at the hospital to make it home except to sleep. He was amazed at how much he missed them and looked forward to seeing them. His colleagues and friends were shocked to learn that he was getting married. To say he was the main conversational topic around the hospital was an understatement.

Although he'd talked long and hard to get his mother to even accept that he was keeping Lily, Grant never doubted she'd take the idea of him marrying and run with it. She'd come through with plans so precise that even the limousine in which they were now riding in to the airport included a car seat.

Sara sat stiffly beside him while her father and Lily sat across from them. Harold was busy keeping Lily entertained with a toy.

Grant looked at Sara's hands, which were clenched so tight in her lap that her knuckles were white. Somewhere inside himself, a place he didn't want to name, hurt that she felt she had no choice but to go through with their ruse of a marriage. Every woman dreamt of her happy wedding day. He had to think of some way of showing his thanks. A way of making this bearable for her.

He reached over and pried one of her hands from the other and intertwined his fingers with hers. At first she tensed but when he didn't let her hand go, she relaxed. Her father glanced at them and smiled then returned to playing with Lily.

Grant leaned over until his shoulder nudged Sara's. He whispered, "Your face says that marrying me is a fate just worse than death."

She gave him a wry smile. "It's better than death."

"Well, that's high praise."

"I'm sorry I can't be more upbeat, but I'll try to do better."

"I look forward to that."

Sara didn't appear any more at ease as they waited to board the plane at O'Hare Airport for their flight to Raleigh, North Carolina. Grant had no idea where his mother had come up with the wedding venue but he was sure it would be appropriate and she'd be there to see that everything went as planned. She would fly Leon and Kim in as well, making the wedding party complete.

"I need to change Lily." Sara pulled the diaper bag over her shoulder and took Lily from her father. "I'll be right back."

Grant watched her walk away.

"I wouldn't worry about it," Harold said. "She is strong. All brides are a little emotional before their wedding."

"I've never seen Sara this...pensive."

"I have. When she had to give the baby she carried over to the parents. She'll come round." Harold walked away, not giving Grant time to ask questions.

In North Carolina, another limousine waited at the airport curb to whisk them away.

Sara watched out the window as they traveled along a highway with green rolling hills on either side. Small colorful farmhouses dotted the landscape every so often. All the serenity of the landscape was in direct contrast to the bubbling anxiety within her.

Was she making a mistake? At least she was helping

a little girl live with someone who wanted her. It wasn't much different than what she'd done for Emily when she'd handed her over to her parents. Lily would have more from Grant than Sara had received from her mother, like feeling wanted. But how would Lily feel when Sara left her? Or Sara had to leave her? That thought didn't improve her feelings. At least Lily was young enough not to wonder if it was because of something she did.

Grant would soon find someone to replace her. She was only temporary anyway. The plan had never been for her to stay for the long haul. That wasn't part of the agreement. Did she want to stay? She glanced at Grant. Maybe she was starting to. It didn't matter. She needed to be wanted for who she was, not for how she could help him.

Grant would find another wife. Why did the idea settle over her like a shroud? He was only interested in making this look like a real marriage for Lily's sake. He'd said nothing about wanting anything more. Sara's heart burned in a way it never had before.

The car pulled into the stone and iron gated drive of a resort. They traveled up a tree-canopied road into an open area with a finely manicured lawn and flowers blooming in patches along it.

She sighed. "Oh, my, it's beautiful."

"I'm glad you like it." Grant smiled. His concerned look was gone.

The driver stopped at the front door of a one-story stone building. Letting go of her hand, Grant stepped out of the car and met the man who came out to greet them. Sara rolled down the window as they spoke and Grant leaned in. "We're staying in cottages located around the property. We'll get out and go by golf cart from here. Mother has already assigned them." He opened Sara's door.

"Your mother is here?"

"She has come and gone. She had to take care of some things in town. We'll see her tonight."

Sara was almost as nervous about meeting Grant's mother as she was about the marriage. She was in way over her head this time.

"You and your father will be staying together."

"What about Lily?"

"She'll be in a nearby cottage. Mother hired a nanny to see to her. You can check on her any time you want. So don't worry," Grant informed her.

Sara wasn't pleased with the idea. She wanted Lily with her but she said, "Okay."

Grant helped her out of the car and into the golf cart. "I'll see you this evening at dinner."

She nodded. Dinner. Where they would all act like this was a real wedding. A love match. But it wasn't. It was pretend. Pretend to be a wife. Pretend to be a mother. Just pretend. The urge to run swamped her.

The attendant drove her and her father along a winding narrow blacktop trail until they came to a sweet, idyllic-looking cottage much like those she'd seen in picture books. It had a small front porch on one side with a white railing, bright yellow siding and a red door. A vine with hot-pink blooms grew along one porch post and up over the roof. It was magical.

The inside didn't disappoint either. There was a small but comfortable sitting room done in a floral print that brought the outside in, a kitchen area and two bedrooms, each with their own bathroom.

"Little girl, I think this room is yours."

"Uh…" Sara stepped into the room where her father already stood.

Hanging from the door of the closet was the most amazing wedding dress and veil she could have imagined. The dress was simple in design, with small straps and a fitted bodice of shimmering gauze that was pulled tight to create folds. The skirt was an overlay of more netting on netting. She touched the dress almost with reverence. Lifting a section, she let it fall, watching the material glistening in the light. The veil was short and trimmed in seed pearls. On the floor were a pair of white slippers.

Her father stepped closer and put his hand across her shoulders, giving her a squeeze. "You're going to be a beautiful bride."

The next few hours went by in a haze. She checked on Lily, whose cottage was within walking distance, then dressed for dinner. Everyone was to meet at the main building.

Although she had brought her finest dress for the occasion, Sara worried that it might not be good enough. However, when she opened the closet in her room she found three dresses, including accessories, hanging there. A note was attached to one. "These are for you. Pick what you like and enjoy."

Her mother-in-law-to-be had thought of everything.

Sara was grateful for the dresses. She chose a classic blue shift and paired it with blue and white shoes. She pulled her hair up to one side with a pin she'd brought from home. Satisfied with how she looked, she and her father rode a golf cart up to the main lodge.

Grant was at the entrance, waiting for them. She was thankful. Somehow he gave her strength. He had to know how nervous she was about all of this. Did he feel the same way?

Her father went in ahead of them.

"You look gorgeous tonight." Grant stood close but didn't touch her.

Unsure, she looked at him. "Thank you. You do too."
That was an understatement. He looked magnificent.

Dressed in a navy suit that almost matched her dress, a
crisp white shirt and a navy, green and yellow striped tie,
he was breathtaking. In another world at another time she
would have pinched herself for being so lucky as to have
him as a husband.

"Shall we go in?" Grant offered his arm.

Accepting it, she said, "I guess so."

He placed his hand over hers, his touch reassuring.

It was a small group that greeted them when they entered the lodge. Her father, the nanny, holding Lily, Leon
and a lady who was dressed impeccably in what had to
have been the latest designer fashion. *Grant's mother.* She
and Grant shared the same eye color and bearing. Sara
looked for more similarities but found none. Grant was
evidently the spitting image of his father. What must he
think each morning when he looked in the mirror?

The woman stepped forward. "Hello. I'm Clarisse
Smythe. It's nice to meet you." Her smile seemed genu-
ine. Would she be wearing the same one if she knew this
wedding was a sham?

Sara returned a smile, hoping it showed more warmth
than she felt. "Hello. It's nice to meet you too. Thank you
for the lovely dresses. My wedding gown is perfect."

Clarisse gave her an air kiss to the cheek. "I'm glad you
like them. Grant gave me a number of suggestions and I
went with them."

Shocked, she looked at Grant. How could he possibly
know her that well in the few short weeks they'd been
living together? Or had he been around women so much
that he just knew what one liked? She suspected it was
the latter.

What did she really know about him? Since this wasn't a real marriage would he be seeing other women after they were married? Would he care if she went out? Heaven help her, she was in a mess. One she was confident would end with her distraught.

Grant said something but she missed it. "What?"

"They're waiting to serve dinner." He took her hand.

She held on. There was security there. What would it be like to have that in her life all the time? To have Grant? That was one road of thought she best not travel.

The next few hours went by in a blur of smiles and conversations that later she couldn't remember having. Kim arrived just before the meal. She gave Sara a huge hug.

All evening Grant continually touched her as if he were a real groom that couldn't get enough of his bride. But she knew better. When she'd agreed to marry Grant she'd not imagined everything seeming so...so normal.

"I would like to make a toast," Grant's mother was saying, "to the woman who finally captured my son's heart."

Sara was grateful for the dim lights hiding the heat on her face.

Everyone lifted their glasses. It took her a moment to join them. Grant leaned over and whispered, "Hang in there," before he kissed her temple.

When dinner was over he walked her to the cart that would take her to her cottage for her last night as a single woman. At least for a while.

"Sleep well, Sara. See you in the morning."

She gave him a wry smile.

Before she went to bed she walked over to check on Lily. She was sleeping soundly and the nanny promised to call if Lily became unhappy. How was she ever going to give up the little girl? But that was the plan. Just as it had been before. She couldn't run this time.

* * *

Despite her trepidation about the next day, Sara slept well. She was woken early by her father's tap on the door. "Little girl, it's your big day."

The ceremony was to take place at ten that morning.

"To catch the best light," Grant's mother had said.

Sara picked at her breakfast when it was delivered. She'd just finished showering when there was a knock at the front door. A maid sent by Grant's mother arrived to help her dress. Soon after, Kim joined them, wearing a pale yellow dress.

"You look wonderful!" Sara exclaimed, holding her at arm's length.

"I'm sure no one will even notice me once they see you. Dr. Smythe, Grant certainly didn't have eyes for anyone but you last night."

Was that true? She'd sure had a hard time keeping herself from staring at him. Surely she would have noticed if he'd been looking at her that much.

"Girl, I can't believe that you're getting married and didn't even tell me you were dating Dr. Delicious. Does he have a friend?"

Sara couldn't help but smile. "I'll ask. I think Leon is available."

Half an hour later, Sara stood in front of the large free-standing mirror, wondering who the person was who was staring back at her. She'd never looked or felt more beautiful. Would Grant think so?

Outside, waiting for her, was a golf cart large enough to accommodate her in the full dress as well as Kim and her father. When Grant's mother had popped in for a moment she'd asked about Lily and had been told that the nanny would have her at the wedding. It was difficult to relinquish control. How was she going to walk away when the time came?

The chapel she and Grant were to marry in was an arching two-story all-glass building surrounded by enormous green fir trees. She was speechless as the driver stopped in front of it. Never had she dreamed of such a perfect wedding site.

Kim alighted from the cart and promptly proceeded down the aisle. Sara took her father's arm and they moved to stand in the doorway. Someone handed her a beautiful bouquet of white roses. The scent swirled around her.

This was too much like for real.

The morning light shone just above the treetops, giving the space a celestial feel. The place was everything she would have dreamed of for a wedding. The rest of the party stood at the end of the aisle flanked by dark wooden benches.

She and her father walked to the front to the sound of a harp.

Grant waited. Dressed in a dark tux with a crisp white shirt, he was Hollywood opening night debonair. The look on his face she would have called love if she hadn't known better.

He stepped forward and offered her his hand.

CHAPTER SEVEN

GRANT WASN'T CERTAIN he drew a breath the entire time it took Sara and her father to join him.

Sara was the most mesmerizing, angelic creature he'd ever seen. A vision in white with her dark hair pulled back and a veil that fell just below her shoulders. Who would have thought that his father would have been indirectly responsible for creating this moment? If Lily hadn't needed a nanny he would have never met Sara.

Her eyelids flickered up then down again as she gave him her hand. It shook.

He escorted her the few steps to the altar.

There Sara gave him a questioning look. He smiled with confidence. They would get through this together. Then came their vows. Hers were spoken softly but to his amazement she held his gaze.

His turn came and his mouth went dry. He had to clear his throat to speak. Somehow each word seemed the perfect one.

The pastor said, "Now for the rings."

Sara's stricken look locked with his. He gave her an encouraging smile.

Leon stepped forward and handed him her ring. He slipped it on her finger and she couldn't seem to take her attention off it. When she looked at him, her eyes shimmered.

How was he supposed to get through the rest of this if she cried?

Sara trembled when Kim nudged her elbow and handed her a ring. A bright smile curved her lips as she took it and placed it on his finger.

"You may kiss your bride," the preacher said.

Grant put his finger under Sara's chin and lifted it until their gazes met. His lips found hers. Her hand came to his waist. She returned his kiss. It seemed to go on forever yet not long enough. When he lifted his head she sighed. His heart squeezed.

Seconds later they were presented as man and wife.

A whirl of activity surrounded them. Clarisse jumped up and hugged first Grant and then Sara before she hurried away, saying something about seeing to the reception. Harold kissed his daughter and shook Grant's hand. The nanny hovered nearby. Lily was making happy sounds. Sara stepped over and took Lily. Leon and Kim both offered their congratulations. A photographer continually clicked her camera. After a few minutes Grant took Lily from Sara and handed her back to the nanny.

"I can take care of her now," Sara protested.

He said, loud enough for the others to hear, "I know you can but I'd like a few moments alone with my bride."

Everyone, including the pastor, took the not-so-subtle hint and left, leaving him and Sara at the altar. Grant clasped her hand and led her to the nearest pew.

"I, for one, would like to sit. I've not been so scared since I opened my first patient." He took a seat and she joined him.

Sara giggled. The sound carried like music in the chapel. The tension she'd worn on her face for the last two days had disappeared.

He cleared his throat, ordering his thoughts. "I know

this was more than you bargained for when you took the nanny job, Sara. But I do want you to know what a beautiful bride you are. Thank you for your sacrifice."

She gave him a small smile. "I'm not sure it's any more than yours."

"Well, that's what we need to do, get into an argument before we leave the church."

"Okay, no argument." She craned her neck, leaving a long delicious amount of skin to tempt him. "This is the most beautiful place for a wedding."

"I can't take any credit for that. My mother saw to everything."

She looked at him again. "Even the rings?"

He gave her a sheepish grin. "Well, not everything."

Sara looked at her left hand. "You made a beautiful choice. I'll enjoy wearing it. Of course, I'll return it when this is all over."

Grant felt like he'd been hit without seeing it coming. Over? "It's yours to keep. It's a gift."

"I don't—"

He didn't want to have this conversation. "Enough about all that. I think we have a brunch to attend."

Grant helped her stand and they walked out hand in hand. A cart decorated in white ribbons and bells awaited them. They returned to the lodge where everyone was gathered to greet them.

A buffet of breakfast food was laid out. Grant noted that Sara ate little but she seemed more talkative and happy than she'd been the day before. The situation wasn't ideal but at least she wasn't miserable. It wasn't what he wanted from her but for now it was enough.

His mother came over to speak to them. "I know there isn't any time for a honeymoon right now because of

Grant's schedule, but I made arrangements for you to use the honeymoon cottage this afternoon and tonight."

She flitted away again.

"We hadn't planned on that," Sara whispered.

No they hadn't discussed the honeymoon but he liked the idea of one. Sara to himself without her caring for Lily or concerned about her father. Maybe they could get to know each other better. He refused to let his thoughts go any further.

"I don't know about you but I could use some peace and quiet, and a nap."

She smiled. "You sure know how to show a girl a good time."

He liked having the real Sara back. And he'd love to show her a good time. But he couldn't push. No doubt she would run if he did.

Kim approached. "I'm going to say goodbye now. Leon's going to take me to catch my plane. His leaves soon after mine. I'll see you soon." She and Sara hugged. "Bye, Mrs. Smythe."

"Mrs. Smythe," Sara whispered. "Sara Smythe."

"Do you like it?"

"Sort of makes me sound important."

Grant leaned close enough that his nose brushed her silky hair. "You are important to Lily and me."

"I just hope I don't disappoint you."

He took her hand. "You couldn't do that. Let's get out of here and go take that nap."

Once again Sara was enchanted by what would be her accommodations for the night. The honeymoon cottage was situated a half a mile from any of the other structures. It faced a pond with a stand of cattails at one end and a swing in front of the cottage. It resembled the one she and her father had stayed in but with white gingerbread trimming on the porch, matching the white of the wood siding. Trees surrounded it on three sides, giving it shade from the noonday sun and a sense of privacy.

Her nerves were shaky at the idea of spending an afternoon and night with only Grant. Lily wouldn't even be there as a barrier between them. What did he expect from her? They hadn't talked about the wedding night. After all, it was a marriage in name only.

Grant helped her out of the golf cart and the man driving told them that if they needed anything to use the phone in the kitchen. With some trepidation, she watched as he drove away. She was now truly alone with Grant.

"I don't know about you but I'd like to get into more comfortable clothes." He was already removing his tux jacket.

She hated to see it go. He'd looked so amazing in it, waiting at the end of the chapel aisle. "What about our clothes? We didn't stop to get them."

He pulled at his bow-tie. "Mother had them moved here for us."

"How nice. I'm not used to this type of service."

"My mother thinks of everything." He opened the first three buttons of his shirt, revealing an appealing sliver of chest.

"I must be sure to thank her."

"Come on. Let's see what she has in store for us inside." He took her elbow.

Sara hesitated. "You know, we never discussed this part of the…arrangement."

Grant looked at her. "Sara, I'm not going to jump you if that's what you're afraid of. Let's just change clothes and relax."

Suddenly she had the need to knock her self-assured

husband off center a little. "Aren't you afraid that I might jump you?"

He grinned at her. "I wouldn't have any complaints if you did."

A ripple of warmth went through her as she walked beside him up the steps.

Inside, the cottage was as lovely as the outside. There was a sitting room, a small kitchen area, and only one large bedroom.

"You can stop the wide-eyed look. I'll sleep out here on the sofa," Grant said.

"I could—"

"Please don't take what gallantry I have left away from me on my wedding day."

The tension in her eased. Grant had a way of doing that for her. "Thank you, sir knight."

Grant's face turned serious. "Sara, don't make the mistake of thinking of me as being knightly. I'm not. I don't live by chivalrous rules so beware. I'll change in the bathroom and you can have the bedroom."

He may not think he did but he was wrong. More than once since she'd met him he'd been fair and helpful. To her, her father and particularly Lily.

As he walked by he lifted his duffle bag off the floor by the handles.

She'd wait until he was done changing so he wouldn't have to stay in the bathroom longer than he wished. There were full-length glass French doors leading off the bedroom. She walked over to them. Outside was a deck with a hot tub. She groaned. This place was all about a couple spending time together and she was with a man she was attracted to but shouldn't have. What was she thinking? She had just married him. How much more involved could she be?

She glanced at the bed. There could be more.

"Hey, what do you see?"

She yelped. Had he seen her looking at the bed?

Grant was now dressed in jeans and a T-shirt that showed his chest to its best advantage. He came to stand behind her. "Wow, a hot tub. I'm going to have to try that. Maybe you would like to join me?"

"I didn't bring a suit."

Chuckling, he said, "I don't think one is expected. After all, this is the honeymoon cottage."

She turned to face him and was met with nothing but cotton-covered chest. She looked up at his face. "Are you making fun of me?"

"No. I just think that since we have to be here we might as well enjoy ourselves. I won't touch you unless you ask. How's that?"

He stepped away and for some reason she felt like all the warmth of the day was going with him. The man was starting to get under her skin and being alone with him wasn't going to make that easier. Sara worked the buttons on the back of her wedding gown free. Reaching as many as she could, she still couldn't get out of the dress. Help was required.

The sound of a glass being set on the kitchen counter said that Grant was still in the cottage.

"Grant?"

"Yeah?"

"I'm going to need some help getting out of this gown."

He stuck his head into the room. "I'm needed for husbandly duty?"

Grant was enjoying the situation far more than she. "Yes, or at least friendly duty."

Strolling toward her, he said, "Turn around."

She presented him with her back.

"My goodness. No wonder you need help. There must be hundreds of these things."

"I think Kim said fifty-three."

"Well, it looks like more than that to me."

The dress pulled gently against her cleavage and waist as he worked. With each movement of his fingers her breath shortened. If he didn't finish soon she'd pass out. As the back opened, she had to hold the dress bodice in place so her breasts remained covered.

"Almost done." Grant's voice had taken on a husky timbre. His exhalations brushed against the skin of her bare back, sending tremors through her. "Finished."

Neither of them moved. Grant's body heat warmed her from behind. Seconds later the pad of a finger traced a line down the small of her back.

A gasp caught in her throat. Time stood still. Then coolness touched her skin.

Seconds later the front door of the cottage was opened then closed.

Grant sensed more than heard Sara join him on the porch. He was stretched out on one of the two matching loungers, trying to rein in his libido. Only with great control had he been able to leave her. He'd come close to slipping his hands along her creamy skin and under her dress until he could cup her breasts in his palms.

The temptation had been more than he could stand and he had touched her. Just an inch or two of that lovely skin but that had been enough to fire the desire he'd been banking since their kiss in his father's den.

Now he was physically in a fix in two ways. One, he was stuck in a honeymoon cottage with nothing to do but pine for Sara. The other was his manhood, standing at throbbing attention with no release in sight. He'd meant it when he'd told her that he wouldn't exert his husbandly rights unless that was what she wished. They had a marriage in name only. She'd given him no indication that she wanted more. As far as he could tell, nothing had changed except a few vows since she'd turned him down a week earlier.

He kept his eyes closed and his breathing even as Sara slipped onto the lounger next to his. "Why're you watching me?"

She made a choking sound. "I wasn't."

"Yes, you were. I felt your eyes on me."

The cushion on her lounger creaked as she shifted. "How do you feel someone's eyes on you?"

"Now I know you were watching me, otherwise you wouldn't be asking a question you already know the answer to."

"I was trying to see if you were asleep. Obviously you weren't."

"I almost was." That was a lie. How could he be when his body was hard as a rock for her? "Why don't you take that nap we talked about then we can check in with Lily and take a walk around the pond."

She didn't say anything but every fiber of his being shouted that she was watching him closely. After a moment he opened one eye a crack. "What're you smiling about?"

"You suggested checking in on Lily. I would have thought I'd be the first one to suggest that."

"The kid is starting to grow on me," he retorted lightheartedly.

"I'm proud of you, Grant."

His eyes opened wide and he captured her gaze. Those simple words filled his chest to almost bursting. He'd rarely heard those words. What would it have been like to hear them from his father? Would he be proud of what his son was doing for Lily? He would like to think so.

Sara's hand rested on the arm of her chair. Taking it, he kissed the back. "Thank you. I appreciate hearing that."

She didn't pull away. Instead, she settled more comfortably and closed her eyes. He watched her for a few minutes in wonderment. There was nothing flashy about her. She was nothing like the women he'd entertained himself with before. Sara was the type of woman he'd like in his life forever. Could he trust her with his heart? That was an idea he was better off not fostering.

Soon he drifted off to sleep with Sara's fingers still firmly in his.

Sara woke to the squeaking sound of something swinging. She looked toward the pond. Grant was gently rocking on the swing, pushing himself with a bare foot. For once he seemed at peace. There was no hurrying out the door to a high-pressured job, brooding mood or anxiety over Lily. When he was off he should be able to enjoy downtime. Sara wanted that for him.

His shoes were sitting beside the steps. The grass was plush enough that she kicked off hers as well and joined him. As she approached he moved over in the seat only enough so that when she sat their thighs met. He ran an arm along the back of the swing. She sensed his fingers close by but he didn't touch her. The man was making it hard for her to remain neutral around him.

"Hey, sleepyhead."

"Hi. How long have you been down here?"

"Just a few minutes."

The sun was starting to dip behind the trees. It was large and orange, reflecting off the lake. They couldn't have been in a more romantic spot. "It'll be dark soon."

"Yes," he agreed, still pushing them slowly back and forth. "Are you hungry? The kitchen is stocked and we can always call the lodge."

"I'm fine for right now."

They continue to swing as darkness closed in. The wildlife chirped and rustled around them. Occasionally a fish jumped in the pond. "It's nice here."

"Mmm…" Grant murmured.

"I guess I'd better go in." Sara put her foot down, stopping the swing.

"Stay. I'll be here with you. I won't let anything happen to you."

She believed him. Knew she was safe with Grant. "Maybe for a few more minutes."

"How old were you when your mother left?"

"Four."

Grant made a hissing sound and pulled her against him, hugging her close. "I'm so sorry you had to live through that. I'm sorry you were so afraid."

She snuggled into him, appreciating his warmth and firm presence, his compassion. Somehow his presence made all the darkness slowly surrounding her go away.

"I can't imagine any mother doing such a traumatizing thing to a child."

"What about a man thrusting a baby into a stranger's hands and leaving?" she teased softly.

He gave her a gentle shake. "I was coming back. You're not going to forgive me for that one, are you?"

"Oh, I've forgiven you. I'm just not going to let you forget it." She glanced at him, only able to see his profile in the dim light.

"Great. I'm going to have to hear about it all the time. Look, a shooting star." Grant pointed just above the treeline.

She leaned forward, searching the sky. "Where? I've never seen a shooting star."

"What? Never?"

"I live in Chicago, remember? It's hard to see the stars for the lights."

He jumped up from the swing, almost knocking her out of it. "Then tonight we will."

Where had his enthusiasm for showing her the stars come from? He was headed for the cottage.

"Grant, what're you doing?" Panic filled her voice.

"Stay put. I'll be right back. I promise."

She believed him. Despite the dark closing in, she was confident he'd return for her. He was as good as his word. A moment later he was back, with the comforter of the bed in his hand.

"It's not that cold out here."

As if he were talking to a small child, he said, "We're not going to put it around us. We're going to lie on it. Come on." He led the way out into the open area away from the cottage.

Sara followed more slowly. Barely visible, he was already fluffing the cover in the air when she joined him. It floated to the ground and he walked around it, adjusting the corners.

"I had no idea star-watching was this much work," she joked.

"Only if you want to do it right." His voice carried in the night air. Her eyes adjusted to the gloom, letting her see the outline of his body. Grant plopped down on the spread and patted the space beside him. "Join me."

She didn't take it as a request but a demand. How like him not to give her a choice. She sat next to him. "So where did you learn how to stargaze?"

"My father used to wake up my brother and me to see

special events in the sky. We would go down the road to where there were no buildings or homes. I haven't thought about that in a long time." There was wonder in his voice.

So his father did have one redeeming quality.

It was almost so dark she couldn't see the treeline.

Grant lay on his back, crossing his arms under his head. "Come on. Lie back. You can't see as well sitting up."

Soon he would become a voice in the night. She did as he said. His body warming her on one side let her know she was safe in the blackness.

As if he knew her thoughts he said, "Relax. I'm right here. I won't leave you."

"I am relaxed."

"No, you're not. I hear the tightness in your voice."

She huffed. "I know you're a good doctor but that's going too far."

He chuckled. "There may not be any scientific truth in it but I know you aren't as uptight as you were a second ago."

She smiled. He was right, she wasn't. "Okay, you win. What do I do?"

"Just look up."

Sara did so. There were a few stars out. With each minute that passed more joined the others. It became so dark she couldn't see her hand in front of her face or make out Grant but the show above was amazing. "It's like nothing I've ever seen before."

"I thought you'd like it." Minutes went by. "Look, there's another shooting star."

"Where?"

He moved beside her. "You have to look quickly or you'll miss it."

She searched the sky. "Will there be more?"

"There might be." His hand brushed her leg.

A tingle of fire went through her. His fingers found

hers and he weaved their hands together. They lay in silence. Suddenly there was a trail of light on the horizon. Sara jerked to a sitting position. "I see one."

"Yes, it is."

"Amazing."

"Lie down. There may be another."

This time when her head went back a muscled arm lay beneath it. She hesitated a moment before she moved in closer to Grant. His hand cupped her shoulder and he pulled her nearer. Aware of every breath he took, she drew pleasure and comfort from having him close.

"Is stargazing one of your usual date activities?"

"No, I only save it for my wives."

"You have had more than one wife?"

"Heavens, no," he said. "For your information, you're the only woman I've ever taken stargazing."

"I learn something new about you all the time."

Grant said in a soft voice, "I know a few things about you. Like you have a huge heart, you speak your mind and you love your father. So what do you know about me?"

"I know you care more about people and family than you want to let on. The last thing you wanted to do was raise a child but you plan to do it to the best of your ability and you like chocolate ice cream."

"How do you know my favorite ice-cream flavor?"

"Do you think you've been eating out of the same carton for the last three weeks? I've been buying a carton at least once a week with the grocery order."

He laughed and tugged her closer. "I noticed. I thought it was sweet. Thank you." His lips found her temple.

Why must he be so nice? She mustn't get caught up in him or Lily. But it would be so wonderful to pretend for just a little while that she had a husband and child. Her own family. What if she did pretend? Who would it hurt but her? Grant's only interest in their marriage was getting custody of Lily but he did seem to find her attractive. Lily was so small she would never know Sara had been her mother for a short while. So what if she passed the time enjoying being married to Grant? When he was done with her they could each move on. She would quietly deal with any heartache it might cause. After all, she'd done it before. She could do it again.

But would it be worth it? Oh, yes. Just to have one more of Grant's kisses…

"There's one." Grant rolled her toward him so that she came across his chest.

There was no seeing the star. She and Grant were face to face. What interested her anyway was the hard body beneath her. She placed a hand on his chest, pushing up so her face was above his. Bringing her mouth down, she aimed for what she hoped was his. She found the corner of it and slipped her lips over to completely cover his. It only took a second for his arms to encase her and pull her fully against him.

To her amazement and with a bolster to her self-esteem, she felt his manhood long and hard between them. Grant's obvious desire fueled her need. A power she'd never known she possessed surged through her. She'd been someone's daughter, a carrier for someone's baby, nurse and nanny. At this moment Grant wanted her for just herself. Was there anything in the world more intoxicating?

She nipped at his bottom lip. A groan from deep within him told her he enjoyed her aggression. To ease the pain she ran the tip of her tongue across the spot. That seemed to inflame him more. He pulled and straightened her over him until the tip of his manhood found the V of her legs. Their jeans were the only barrier to ultimate satisfaction.

It was no longer her kiss but his when he teased the seam of her mouth with his tongue. Her hands came up to bracket his face as she opened for him. Had she ever been kissed like this before? Would she be again? Widening her mouth, she opened, greeting him like a long-lost friend. Grant's tongue thrust in the most erotic manner, causing her to squirm against him. A fire of need grew deep within her. Joining him in the fury of their tongues mating, she let him guide her into releasing to taste again.

She hummed with desire.

Grant wasn't sure what had happened to make Sara kiss him but if he'd known stargazing would have this effect on her he would've taken her to the Alder Planetarium days ago.

At this rate they were both going to combust. Yet he wanted to savor her, and their night. Not have her regret it. Pulling back, he pushed her hair away from her face, placing slow kisses to her lips. This did little to help him regain control over the locomotive of desire barreling through him. He rolled Sara onto her back and continued to kiss her eyes, cheeks and chin.

Some time later he gasped, "Sweetheart, if we don't slow down I'm afraid I'm going to embarrass myself with my lack of control. I want this to be memorable between us but for the right reasons."

She wiggled, teasing him. He liked this side of her. Sara continued to surprise him. Each fascinating facet turned him on more than the next. "Let's go inside where I can see you."

Sara stilled. His kiss found her neck this time. If she changed her mind he was afraid he might never recover.

Cupping her face in his hands, he found her lips and it felt as if the sun was shining brightly as his met hers.

She pulled him closer, begging for more.

If he didn't move now he would take her there on the ground, but first he wanted to see her, savor her. He broke away carefully and stood. The moon was rising and there was just enough light for him to see Sara's uplifted face. There was a hopeful, unsure look there.

Grant reached out a hand. It took a second longer than he'd have liked for her to take it. He needed to get her to the bedroom quickly before she could overthink the ramifications of what they were about to do.

Sara slowly came to her feet. When she was beside him, he brought her against his chest, holding her tight. He kissed her until she moaned and then released her, determined to leave her wanting more. Taking her hand, he started toward the cottage. He silently cursed himself for going so far out in the field.

"What about the blanket?" she asked.

That was his Sara, always practical. "We'll get it in the morning." He stopped where they were and pulled her to him, caressing her cheek with his lips. "Can't get enough of you."

"I like that idea."

Her statement only incited the banked hunger burning in him. As abruptly as he'd stopped he started again, bringing her along with him as gently as his need allowed. To his great relief they reached the cottage a minute later.

Inside, he turned on a light switch. The two lamps in the living area came on. Letting go of Sara's hand, he turned to her. For seconds they looked at each other. Sara's hair was tousled and her eyes luminous. She was an amazing creature.

In spite of his arousal he wanted things to go slowly between them so that their first time together wouldn't be stilted or, worse, regretted. "Are you hungry?"

CHAPTER EIGHT

SARA HAD A hard time not to burst out laughing. She couldn't believe Grant was talking about food at a time like this. It was as if the hot, passionate time between them in the last fifteen minutes hadn't happened.

Had he changed his mind? Was the big, strong man, who always knew his mind and went for it, suddenly unsure?

She smiled, locking gazes with him. "I am. For you."

The predatory grin he gave her sent white-hot desire flowing to her center. Boldness with men had never been her strong suit. She'd had boyfriends but none of them had caused her body to vibrate with need as Grant's did. He made her feel daring and sexy. As if she was not only needed but wanted as a woman. She craved him and this time with him. She'd worry about tomorrow when tomorrow came.

She took Grant's hand and tugged him toward the big honeymoon bed.

He grinned. "I like this side of you."

"Oh, there's more to come."

His low growl said he was looking forward to that.

She didn't get to maintain control long. Grant seized her and pulled her onto the bed. As his head lowered he said, "Now, where were we?"

Excitement surged through her. His mouth nuzzled her neck, finding and worshiping the sweet spot below her jaw. As the tip of his tongue touched her heated skin her fingers kneaded his back. His hands moved to her waist and slowly worked their way up her sides to her rib cage until his thumbs rested below her breasts.

She squirmed. When would he touch her? Her nipples hardened and pushed against the thin covering of her bra.

Grant's mouth continued to make magical, amazing moves across her hairline and down to her brow. Still his hands didn't move.

With her hands at his waist, she pushed his shirt up and slipped them beneath. Warm skin over hard muscle greeted her. Reveling in the feel of him, she let her fingers have free rein to explore.

Still Grant's hands remained where they were. She groaned and his mouth met hers in a wet, hot kiss. His hips brushed against hers. If the goal was to let her know how much he desired her he'd made his point.

One of Grant's thumbs slowly brushed over her nipple. She jumped. Blood pooled hot at her center, making her throb. Again he touched her and a whimper rolled from her lips. She gripped his back. The man made her weak with longing.

He rolled to his side. His gaze captured hers. "I have to touch you."

Grant's hands gathered her shirt up and his fingers moved underneath to settle on her flesh. She tingled throughout as a hand traveled to the barrier of her bra. Like a pro, he soon located the front clasp and flicked it open. For a fleeting moment she noted that this wasn't his first time of removing a woman's underclothing. That thought vanished as Grant's hand caressed her breast. She hissed.

He teased her already sensitive nipple, making it stand

more firmly against his palm. Using his finger, he circled it and moved away to return again. With each touch her breath caught.

"I have to taste you." Grant pushed the material higher.

Sara lifted her torso off the bed enough for him to remove her shirt. With that done, she lay back. Grant hovered over her, his attention on her alone.

"More beautiful than I imagined."

He'd been thinking of her? *Her. He saw her.*

Cupping a breast, he lifted it. Slowly his head came down.

Sara held her breath in anticipation. She shivered the second his mouth drew her in. Molten heat shot to her center as he rolled and tugged her nipple with his tongue. Her fingers tangled in his hair as she accepted all the pleasure he offered.

His attention moved to her other breast and tormented it until she squirmed. His lips traveled to her cleavage, leaving butterfly kisses in their wake. One of his hands massaged the top of her thigh while his mouth journeyed down along her stomach. Her skin rippled with each touch. His mouth paused at the waistband of her jeans. The hand on her thigh slid up, undid the button and gently opened the zipper.

Grant's mouth returned to hers for a smoldering kiss while his hand at her waist flattened over her stomach and slowly slipped beneath her jeans. Sara gasped. Blood roared in her ears. His hand continued until it had moved beneath her panties. There it stopped to brush her curls.

His lips remained on hers, stoking the fire in her until she squirmed. He nibbled at her ear as his index finger teased her mound. Her legs opened of their own volition. Grant took advantage of the offer and slipped his finger into her center. She writhed with the need for his touch.

He returned his mouth to hers and thrust his tongue as his finger mirrored the motion.

Sara's back bowed as her hips flexed and she came undone. This time she was the star shooting out of this world on the sweet bliss of release.

She'd never been more aware of the power of a single touch.

If Grant had this influence over her with just the use of a finger, what would it be like to have him inside her?

Grant pulled his mouth and hand away. "You are amazing."

"I think I should be the one saying that."

His chest seemed to swell with pleasure. "It's time for the clothes to go."

"You're wearing the most. You first," she mumbled.

Grant stood. Pulling his wallet from his back pocket, he found a small square package and laid it on the bedside table before shucking his clothes. Sara should have known by how uninhibited he'd been during their meeting in the bathroom that he'd feel no compunction about undressing in front of her.

In the dim light coming from the other room she could see he was a striking example of male anatomy. Wide shoulders, muscled chest, lean waist and solid thighs made him seem like an athlete. Her gaze settled on his manhood, which stood proud and tall. All for her.

Grant took her by both wrists and tugged her up to stand in front of him. In a low seductive voice he said, "Now it's your turn."

"Grant, I…"

He brushed the outside curve of her breast. "Beautiful. Please share with me."

Taking a deep breath, Sara shimmied out of her jeans,

letting them fall to the floor and leaving her naked accept for her panties.

"I want to see all of you." This time his hand went to her shoulder and glided along the back of her arm to her elbow.

With shaking hands, she hooked her thumbs in the lace of her panties and slipped them off.

"How could you ever imagine I wouldn't think you're amazing?" Grant pulled her to him, his hardness a contrast to her softness. His kiss was slow, gentle, and thorough.

Grant made her feel beautiful. As if he saw who she really was.

While he kissed her his hands stroked her skin. As sensitive as her flesh had been before, now that she was unclothed it tingled with the need for his attention from the top of her head to her toes. A caress was a mighty thing. He pulled her close.

Grant's manhood was a ridge of desire standing strong between them. His mouth left hers to kiss the length of her neck out to her shoulder. She purred with ecstasy.

Releasing her, he stepped to the bed and pulled the sheet back. He lay down on his side with his head propped on his hand. With the other, he patted the space beside him. "Please join me."

This was the time when she could say she had changed her mind. Grant wouldn't push. He would be disappointed but he'd never take her against her will. Need, and something she wasn't willing to label drove her to slide along the cool sheet to lie facing him.

Grant's hand came to rest on her hip. She smoothed a hand over his chest, memorizing all the dips and rises. There was a dusting of hair on his pectorals and she enjoyed playing with the springy mass. She looked at Grant. He watched her. His focus went to her breasts. As his finger touched the tip of a nipple his eyes became almost as dark as the night.

Lowering her hand, Sara ran it over the hard plane of his stomach, bumping the tip of his manhood. He sucked in a breath. Using the back of her hand, she lightly brushed down his length. She was captivated when it quivered. Looking at him, she saw a man straining for control. It gave her a heady sense of power to know that Grant wanted her so badly.

"Now you've done it," he rumbled. Plucking the packet from the table, he opened it and rolled the condom over his shaft. He pushed her shoulders back against the sheets and leaned down to kiss her. Only his lips touched hers. Not enough, she wanted more. All of him.

She pulled him to her. He settled between her legs. His length rested at her opening. She shifted her hips, taking the tip of him. Still she wanted more.

"Grant," she moaned in desperation. Why was he teasing her when she was so hungry to have him?

Her gaze met his as he whispered, "Tell me what you want."

"You." The word was barely out before his mouth claimed hers and his shaft did as well. She bucked off the bed then settled as he found a rhythm that she joined. It wasn't long until she soared above their merged bodies and drifted down on a satisfied sigh.

Grant flexed his hips with force, going deep three more times. A guttural groan announced the summit of his pleasure. He lowered himself to lie over her, relaxed and heavy. Seconds before she would have complained of his weight, he rolled to his side. His arms remained around her and he kissed her temple.

They lay together until their breathing evened again.

Life had just taken an irreversible turn. She'd never have enough of Grant. Exhaling, she drifted off to sleep.

Sara reached for him in the middle of the night and Grant was powerless to refuse her, neither did he want to. This time their coming together was sweet and slow, nothing like the frenzy of earlier. He'd never been more flattered than when Sara had found her release.

Just listening to her soft even breathing next to him gave him a sense of contentment he'd never felt before. He didn't make it a habit of spending the night with women but something seemed right about having Sara's soft body snuggled against his.

She was as big-hearted in her lovemaking as she was about everything else in her life. He wished he'd had her in his world when he'd been growing up. She would have been supportive and encouraging. With Sara he measured up. Was good enough. That emotion had been missing in his life where his relationships were concerned. He liked this new feeling.

The hazy morning light shone through the curtains as he eased from the bed, making an effort not to disturb Sara. She had earned her rest. He grabbed his phone and as quietly as possible he opened the door to the outside deck where the hot tub was located. After making a quick call to check on Lily, he flipped the switch on the wall on and slipped into the water. The warm jets of liquid churning around him felt magnificent, but not as wonderful as having Sara in his arms.

Grant closed his eyes. His life had changed by a one-eighty turn in less than a month. He was a father and now a husband. Neither of those had been in his plans. To his amazement he didn't want to run from either. That was because of Sara. But he couldn't let himself get too close to her. He wouldn't trust her with his heart. He had done that once and had the scars to prove it. But Sara was nothing like Evelyn. She would never do to him what Evelyn had. Could he expose his heart to Sara? Would it be worth the chance of rejection?

The click of the door opening brought his eyelids up.

"Hey," Sara said as she closed the door behind her. She was wearing his shirt. It was far too large but he'd never seen any woman look more adorable. His body was already reacting to her. How was he supposed to think straight if he was in a constant state of arousal when he was around her?

She seemed unsure, as if she didn't know what her reception would be. This morning-after business could make or break a relationship and he wouldn't let that happen between them. When had he become so interested in a relationship? Since the moment Sara had so freely expressed her pleasure at his touch. For her, he'd done everything right.

Sara came closer. "I need to call and check on Lily. We didn't do that last night."

Grant stood and her eyes widened. He smiled. "I had other things on my mind."

Pink came to her cheeks.

He liked it that he could make her blush. "I called a few minutes ago. She's doing fine." He took that second of weakness to grab her hand and pull her toward him.

She resisted his tug. "I'll ruin your shirt."

"I'll get another."

"But…" She relented and joined him in the water.

"But what?" he said as he pulled her against his chest, sat on the bench and settled her on his lap. One of her arms came to rest along the back of his shoulders.

"Don't we need to be thinking about getting back to Chicago today?"

"I'm thinking about something else." His lips found hers.

Some time later, Grant watched as Sara rushed to get all her belongings back into her suitcase. They had spent a leisurely and very memorable time making love before sharing an equally relaxing breakfast. Now, for some reason, Sara seemed a little anxious.

Grant caught her on one of her passes to the bathroom to get something. He guided her down to sit beside him on the bed. "Hey, what's going on?"

"Nothing. I'm just trying to get ready to go." She wouldn't look at him.

"I think there's more to it than that." She didn't say anything. Worry crept into his chest, tightening it. "Come on, Sara, talk to me."

"I don't know. It's just that everything seems so surreal."

"What's not real? For me last night was about as real as it gets."

She continued to look at the dresser in front of them. "You know what I mean."

"Yes, sweetheart, it's all new to me too."

"Please don't call me that. You know I'm not your sweetheart. This is just a business agreement. I'm just the nanny with benefits."

That was like a breathtaking thump to his chest. It hurt. "That's pretty harsh."

Giving him a pointed look, she asked, "So how would you explain our relationship?"

What was she fishing for? For him to say how much in love with her he was? He'd done that before and what had it gotten him? Evelyn had dumped him and married his father. No, he wasn't going there, even to keep Sara in his bed. He had to tread lightly here.

"I don't know. Who do we have to explain it to? This is between us."

"I'm sorry, Grant. I'm just not sure I'm good with that."

So much for smoothing into the morning after. He stood and looked down at her. Now she studied the floor, hands clasped in her lap. "Just for the record, last night was damn fine. I would love to repeat it any time you're willing but I won't put strings on you where that's concerned. When you figure out how you want things to be, let me know." He picked up his already packed bag. "I'll be waiting outside."

Sara hadn't meant to hurt Grant's feelings. Or make an already strained situation more stressful. He'd been rejected so many times in life that she didn't want to damage his ego. Grant deserved better than that.

Still, she had to protect herself. They weren't in a permanent relationship. She was terrified that if she let go and opened her heart she'd be far more shattered than she could handle when they parted ways. She cared for Lily but Grant had pushed his way past her defenses and made her want him in and out of bed. She'd told herself it would just be for a while last night, and now she dared to wish for forever. But that wasn't going to happen.

Finishing her packing, she joined him on the porch. The driver was there, placing Grant's bag in the golf cart. She was relieved to have a buffer between her and Grant. At least they wouldn't be alone again until they were home. Home. Grant's father's house wasn't her home, even though technically she'd be the mistress of the household.

Grant glanced at her. She hated that disappointed look in his eyes.

The driver came up the steps for her bag and went down

again. Grant started to follow but she grabbed his hand. "I'm sorry. I'm just tired."

He smiled at her and squeezed her hand. "We didn't get much sleep. Don't worry, we'll figure this out together." He didn't release her hand as they stepped onto the cart.

That was the first time Grant had implied that they were really a couple. She glanced back at the cottage. It had been a perfect night and morning. If only the real world was not just around two more turns.

Her father, Grant's mother and the nanny, with Lily in her arms, were all waiting beside two limousines in front of the lodge. They were all smiles and Sara managed to plaster one on as well. Grant helped her out of the cart.

Grant's mother came forward to hug and air kiss him. Grant shook hands with Sara's father.

"Nice to have you as part of the family," her father said.

Sara winced. With each day that went by it would be harder to explain this to her father. Grant turned to his mother. "I wish we had more time, Mother, but our plane leaves at eleven so we need to be going."

"I know. I'll see you again soon."

Sara stepped toward her. "Thank you, Ms. Smythe, everything was lovely."

"It was a beautiful wedding, wasn't it?"

"Yes, it was," Sara agreed. If she and Grant had loved each other it would have been perfect.

"We have to go." Grant ushered her to the front car while her father and the nanny took the other one.

When they were settled beside each other and the car was moving down the drive Sara asked, "Why aren't my father and Lily riding with us?"

"I guess my mother thought we might want a few more moments alone."

Sara didn't comment on that.

Grant put his arm around her shoulders and she laid her head back. As conflicted as her emotions were, the feel of Grant's strong chest beneath her cheek made her feel secure.

"Try to get some sleep on the way to the airport. We'll be back to dealing with Lily after that."

"Sara…" Grant's voice woke her. "We're at the terminal." She'd slept the entire drive in his arms. What would it be like to do that always? She couldn't think that way. It wasn't healthy for her, Grant or Lily. She wouldn't think about that. Instead, she'd concentrate on enjoying the now and deal with the future when it came.

They arrived home close to Lily's bedtime. Grant had stopped on the way from the airport to pick up takeout for dinner. They sat around the table. Everyone she loved most in the world was there, with the exception of her father, who they had dropped off at his house.

Loved. She looked at Grant. She did love him. Why had she let that happen? Because she'd had no choice. Grant hadn't given her one.

She left the table, using the excuse of putting Lily to bed.

"I'll be along to help after I clean up here." Grant pushed back his chair.

"I can take care of Lily. I'm sure you need to check in at the hospital."

Grant studied her for a long moment then nodded. Did he understand that she needed some time to herself?

Grant wasn't sure what had happened at the dinner table but something wasn't right with Sara. He'd known the convenient marriage idea would be difficult for both of them but he hadn't had another solution. He had pulled Sara in further than he'd intended and now he was having a hard time keeping emotional distance. In fact, he wasn't going to let her run from him.

He had no intention of spending any night under the same roof with her and not be sharing the same bed. The days of him sleeping on the sofa or hiding out at his apartment were over. She'd been more than receptive to his lovemaking last night and that morning. He refused to let her hide from him now. There was something between them that was worth exploring.

Grant took his time going upstairs. He wanted Sara to have some space before he joined her. He entered his bedroom and went to the bathroom. No sound came from Sara's room. He showered, then pulled on his boxers before tapping on their adjoining door. There was no response. He knocked again and opened the door a crack.

"Is there something wrong?" To his surprise, Sara was sitting on the bed, facing the door, as if she was expecting him. She was wearing the gown with the thin straps he'd wanted to pull off her weeks ago.

"No. I'm just checking on you." That was a half-truth. He wanted her, wanted her badly, and had every intention of having her.

"I'm fine."

He strolled around to the other side of the bed.

"What're you doing?" She twisted on the mattress, watching him.

"I'm getting into bed with my wife." He pushed his boxers down. He enjoyed her hiss of surprise. "After all, we are married and this is my bedroom."

"No, it isn't!"

He climbed under the covers and grinned at her. "Yes,

it is. You've been sleeping in my childhood bedroom all this time."

Her mouth dropped open. "Why didn't you say something?"

He shrugged. "At first it didn't matter and after a while I sort of enjoyed the thought of you asleep in my bed."

Sara picked up a pillow and threw it at him.

"Two can play that game." He snatched the pillow from behind him and tossed it at her.

She giggled and went after another one. Grant grabbed it out of her hand and captured her wrist, dragging her to him. Sara fell across his chest. Pleasure hot and strong flowed through him. He had Sara in his arms again. He rolled her over and kissed her. Her hands found his back and pulled him to her. This was how it should be between them always.

CHAPTER NINE

FOR SARA, DURING the next week the household settled into a rhythm that was both comforting and dreamlike at the same time. Grant would grab a quick coffee with her and Lily before he left each morning. It would all be very domestic and normal appearing except he never gave her a goodbye kiss. It was as if both of them associated that intimate act with a real marriage. Which theirs wasn't. And wouldn't be, no matter how she wished it so.

Her days were spent taking care of Lily's needs just as before. She looked forward to the evenings and seeing Grant far too much. They would agree in the morning what they would do for dinner. Sometimes she cooked, others he brought something home, but either way she was always glad to see him.

If she was cooking he spent time entertaining Lily. He was becoming a good father, all things considered. If he was making dinner, he wanted her to sit in the kitchen with the baby and talk to him while he put everything on the table. Next to his lovemaking, she would miss their evenings together. With great effort she tried not to dwell on that fast-approaching day but that was easier said than done. When the time came, where would she go to recover from her broken heart? What would she do?

Grant helped her get Lily down for the night when he

didn't have work to see to. With Lily asleep and his work finished, they would watch a few TV shows in the den, with him seated in the corner of the sofa and she curled into his side.

Then came her favorite part of the day when Grant saw to her pleasure as if it was the most important thing he had done all day. During their lovemaking she felt taken care of instead of the one doing the nurturing. She went to sleep securely wrapped in his arms.

One day Grant had a late surgery case. He called to let her know. Sara went to bed without him but it didn't seem right. She was coming to depend on Grant just for her rest. That scared her.

Early in the wee hours, he slipped into bed and gathered her close. She placed her hand over one of his. "How did it go?"

"Successful. You should be asleep."

"I will now."

Had he murmured, "I missed you too," before he'd kissed her cheek and his breathing had become even?

At breakfast later in the week Grant said, "I'd like to take you out tonight."

"I don't know. What about Lily?"

"Your father's going to watch her. Lily can sleep in the bassinet until we get home. As long as Harold doesn't have to go up the stairs, he's assured me he can handle it."

She turned from the sink. "So you've planned all this out?"

"I have. We're married but have never been on a date. That seems wrong somehow. I'd like to correct that tonight."

"Where're we going?"

He stepped toward the door. "That's a surprise. Just

wear one of those dresses that you told me mother bought you. Be ready at seven."

"But that's Lily's bathtime."

"Come on, Sara, quit making excuses. She can go without a bath for one night."

"But I'm her nanny."

He walked toward her and into her personal space. "Tonight you're my wife. Be ready at seven."

The man she'd met the first day had returned. He wasn't going to accept any more arguments.

Sara watched as Grant skillfully drove through the evening traffic into Chicago. They were traveling along Shore Line Drive when she asked again where they were going.

He took her hand and held it. "We're almost there."

Grant looked superb dressed in a light blue collared shirt, tan slacks and navy sports jacket. He had even had a haircut. Before they'd left he'd complimented her on her looks as they first appraised each other. She had chosen the A-line dress with flowers around the hemline and paired it with a pink wrap. Feeling good about her appearance, she had practically glowed from his admiration. He'd looked as if he could eat her up. Stepping across the space between them, he'd kissed her forehead. "You look amazing, Mrs. Smythe."

Now he was steering his sports car into the entrance of the Adler Planetarium on the shore of Lake Michigan.

"I've not been here since a school field trip when I was ten," she said.

"I think it'll be a little different than that tonight."

Everything was altered when Grant was around.

Holding hands, they walked into the building. At the desk Grant gave his name and they were directed down a hall. Their footsteps echoed in the large room. At the single glass door, he pushed it open and let her go ahead of him. They were outside again on a triangular terrace that faced the water. In the middle of it sat a table covered in a white cloth with two place settings. A candle flickering in a globe between them. Nearby stood a waiter in a white and black uniform.

"This is wonderful." She looked at Grant.

He was observing her with a smile on his face. "I thought you might like this. After dinner we'll go look at the stars without lying on the ground."

"I rather enjoyed seeing them that way."

His hand came to her back and he pulled her to his side for a quick hug. "I did too. Especially what happened afterward."

Sara wished that it could always be like this between them. With each passing day she grew more in love with him and Lily but she was living in a fantasy world. It was all pretend. Not once had Grant indicated he felt anything other than friendship for her. He enjoyed her body but that was as far as his emotions went. He trusted her with Lily and his pleasure but not his heart. She hated Evelyn and his father for causing him to shut off emotionally.

Even if she could convince Grant they could make something of their marriage, did she really think she deserved to have him and Lily in her life? How long would she stay?

She wouldn't think about that now. It was a beautiful night. She had a handsome man to enjoy it with and she was going to take advantage of the happiness she could have.

Grant held her chair as she sat then took his own across the table from hers. The waiter approached with a bottle of champagne. As he poured Sara looked out at the lights of Chicago reflecting off the water and back at the formally set table. Finished with his chore, the waiter quietly backed away.

"If this is your usual fare for a first date, I can't imagine what the second date looks like."

"I've never brought anyone here before. For a first or second date."

"Really?"

"Really."

Delight filled her. He was doing something special for her. Something that she could remember as theirs only. It made the night extraordinary.

Grant raised his glass for a toast. "To Sara, the most amazing woman I know."

She couldn't help but blush under his praise as she brought her glass up to touch his.

A few minutes later they were served dinner of filet mignon, seasoned potatoes and green beans wrapped in bacon. The food was divine and cooked impeccably. They made small talk about the weather, Lily and her father's new house.

Putting his fork down, Grant leaned back in his chair. "I haven't taken time to tell you how much I appreciate all you've done. I couldn't have taken care of Lily without you."

"You've told me more than once but it's nice to hear. You've been pretty great also. Especially to my father. Lily."

"I don't know what I'll do if I lose her." Pain filled his voice.

The same as she'd felt when she'd had to give up Emily. Her hands started to tremble and she set her glass down. Why did he bring this up now? "You'll think you want to die."

Grant was watching her closely. "Is that how you felt when you had to give up the baby you carried?"

"Yes. That and more. I made the fatal mistake of becoming too attached. Letting myself start to believe that Emily was mine. It almost killed me to give her up. And I wanted to kill to keep her."

Grant stood and came around the table. He took her hand and brought her to her feet before he enveloped her in a hug. "I'm sorry."

This embrace was about two people who had been wounded, who understood each other's hurt. Sara buried her face in his chest and wrapped her arms tightly around him, letting Grant absorb her pain. He'd come to know her so well in such a short time. No other man she'd ever been involved with had seen her as Grant did.

She finally released him. "We'd better finish our lovely meal."

Grant waited until she was seated again and then returned to his chair.

"I don't want to upset you but I'd like to know—do you ever see or hear from the couple?"

"No, because that's the way I want it. The only way I could or can deal with my feelings is to have nothing to do with Emily or my friends. With that choice came guilt."

"So you haven't seen or heard from your friends since Emily was born?"

Sara pulled on the ends of her napkin, not looking at Grant. "They left messages but I couldn't bear to answer. They have finally given up."

"How long has that been?"

"Five years."

"That must be tough."

"It is. I want to call them but what if I can't handle it?"

"But what if you can?" he said quietly.

"Guilt eats at me for how I've acted. The more time that goes by the harder it is to approach them. I'm afraid that if I see Emily again I'll have to suffer through that agony all over again."

"I think maybe your heart is too big for your own good. And look at what I talked you into. Marrying me so I could keep Lily."

Sara looked off over the water at the lights of Chicago and back to Grant with his wavy hair, perfect mouth and determine jawline. *Yes, but I have had this time with you.* "Enough about my woes. So what's for dessert?"

He lowered his chin giving her a speculative look. "It's time to change the subject, I gather."

She nodded. "I do like my sweets."

"I can take a hint." He raised his hand to the waiter. "And you should have one."

Sara was relieved he was willing to move on and not question her further. She wanted to remember this as a happy night. They finished their chocolate pie à la mode with the only light being the lone candle on the table. It was the most romantic dinner she could have imagined.

"This has been wonderful." Sara placed her fork on the empty plate. "Thank you."

"We're not done." Grant pushed back his chair.

"I can't eat any more."

"I mean we still have a show to go to." He stood.

"Show?"

"We're going to look at the stars through the telescope." There was a note of excitement in his voice.

"I've never done that before."

He smiled down at her. "Then this will be a big night for you."

And it was. She was enjoying having his complete attention. Being charmed by him.

Grant came around the table and helped her out of her seat. They walked hand in hand into the building and down the hallway. He led her to a doorway that opened into a large room with a huge telescope positioned in the middle of it.

"Does everyone get to do this?" she asked.

"Well, not everyone. I'm a member and a big supporter so I get a few perks that others don't."

"That figures."

A man beside the wall pushed a button. The roof of the ceiling slowly opened. He soon left.

"Come over here and look through this." Grant directed her to a pedestal chair beside the telescope. "Put your eye right here." He pointed to an eyepiece. "Close the other one."

She did as instructed. There were pinpoints of light in the sky. More than she'd seen on their honeymoon night.

"Now, use this." Grant took her hand and placed it on a knob on the arm of the instrument. "Roll it back and forth until what you see becomes sharp and clear." His hand remained on hers and his body surrounded her with warmth. She was safe.

"Sara, are you listening to me?"

"Yeah." She moved the knob. The sky became filled with hundreds of thousands of bright lights. She held her breath in amazement. "I thought it was pretty cool to see all the stars out in the field but this is unreal."

"It is pretty grand."

Over the next hour Grant showed her some of his favorite stars, even rattling off their names. "I have one more to show you."

She moved away from the telescope, giving him room to look into the viewfinder. After making some adjustments with the knob, he stepped back. "Okay, I want you to look straight ahead at the star just to the right of the brightest."

Sara looked into the eyepiece. "Got it. What am I looking at?"

"My favorite star. Sara."

Her heart leaped forward a beat. She pulled back and looked at him. "What?"

"I named it after you. It's even official. I have a certificate at home."

She threw her arms around his neck. "What a lovely gift. Thank you."

"I thought maybe it would help you to know that you had a bright light up above whenever you're afraid of the dark."

"It's the nicest gift I've ever received." She kissed him with all the love she had in her heart.

When she pulled away Grant groaned. "On that note I think it's time for us to go home."

Sara gave him a smile of encouragement. "I don't have a problem with that."

As they headed toward Highland Park Sara thought back over their wonderful evening. She wished there could be more. Her star wasn't visible in the glow from the lights of the city but she knew it was there. It would be there when she needed it most. When she had to leave Grant and Lily.

The next Wednesday Grant went to work early so he could return home before noon to get ready for the custody hearing. Leon had assured him that he needn't worry about the hearing, telling Grant that it should be straightforward. Regardless, Grant was nervous. What if he lost Lily? Then he'd lose Sara as well. That just couldn't happen. He couldn't imagine his world without them both in it.

His life had been disrupted and in turn he'd done the same to Sara's. Their marriage, no matter how much he was enjoying his time with Sara, especially physically, was still just a business deal. One he'd paid her handsomely for. She had only agreed to it to give her father a place to live. She was getting what she wanted from the arrangement.

They had both wanted something and had received mutual compensation. Or at least that's what he told himself. It was much easier than admitting that he might be falling in love with her. Though "might" wasn't the right word. He cared for Sara far more than he'd ever cared for Evelyn. He'd never met a more giving woman in his life. Both in and out of bed.

When he made it upstairs to change he found Sara in Lily's room. She was humming softly as she rocked and looked down into Lily's face. They belonged together. Would Sara consider staying longer? Maybe forever? As the nanny?

"Hey." He stepped further into the room.

"Hi."

"What's going on?"

"She was a little fussy. I was just taking a moment to calm her. I think she knows that something important is happening today. Babies sense things."

Grant stepped closer. "Are you worried?"

"A little. How about you?"

"Some, but I'm pretty confident. Leon says it should go our way." That was how he thought of it now, as something he and Sara were doing together. "I'll get dressed and then take her off your hands so you can change."

"Okay." Sara looked down at Lily again, as if he'd been dismissed from her mind.

An hour later they were on their way to the Chicago courthouse. Lily was asleep in the car seat. Sara had dressed her in a fancy one-piece outfit and even added a matching headband with a bow. If it had been him alone, the child would have been lucky to have on a sleeping onesie. Women just seemed to think of things like dressing up a child. Lily would look like the well cared-for, happy baby girl she was to the judge.

Once parked, they opted for taking out the stroller. Sara's argument was that if Lily needed to sleep they had a place to put her. The three of them entered the courthouse building looking like a real family. With a start, Grant realized he thought of them that way.

Leon was there to greet them. "We'll be meeting in the judge's chambers. The Armsteads are here with their lawyer. To tell you the truth, I'm surprised to see them. I hadn't expected them to push the issue this far after they found out you'd married. This may not be the walk in the park I had anticipated."

A pang of fear shot through Grant. "What do I need to do?"

"Both of you…" Leon looked at Sara as well as him "…just need to answer the judge's questions truthfully."

The judge's assistant opened the door and directed them into the judge's personal chambers. Grant held the door as Sara pushed Lily into the office. The Armsteads and their lawyer were already seated in front of a large desk. Three empty chairs were further over. Sara went to the furthest one, pushed the stroller up next to it and sat. Grant took the one next to her and Leon the one closest to the Armstead party.

"I understand that we're all here to decide who should have custody of Lily Evelyn Smythe," the judge said from the other side of the desk.

Sara placed a hand over Grant's where it gripped the

arm of the chair. He glanced at her. She gave him a reassuring smile.

The judge stood and looked over the desk at Lily. "So this is the child in question."

"Yes, sir, it is." Leon began to outline Grant's case.

The judge waved his hand, stopping him. "If you don't mind I'd like to hear from the…" he looked down at the file in front of him "…the Armsteads first."

Grant tensed and Sara squeezed his hand. He turned his over and clasped hers.

Over the next few minutes the Armsteads' lawyer outlined the reasons why they should get custody of Lily.

"Enough of that," the judge said. "I'd like to talk to the couple in question. Please tell me why you believe you are the best choice to be parents of this child."

Mr. Armstead pointed out all of the advantages to living with them. Thankfully he said nothing that Grant wasn't expecting.

The judge asked, "Mrs. Armstead, do you have anything to add?"

She looked at her husband and then shook her head.

The judge turned to Grant. "Dr. Smythe, I would like to hear from you now."

Again Sara clasped his hand tighter. He cleared his throat. "Sir, the important thing here is what is best for Lily. She is my sister but now also my daughter. I believe that she should live with me and my wife, her closest family." He continued to share all he could offer Lily.

As if Lily wanted to give her opinion, she whimpered in the stroller. Grant stopped talking while Sara picked Lily up and held her across her chest, patting her bottom.

Grant look at her. "She needs a change?"

Sara nodded.

He turned to the judge. "Would you excuse us a minute while we see to Lily?"

The judge nodded. Grant stepped past Leon and around the chairs to retrieve the diaper bag from under the seat of the stroller and pulled out a diaper. Sara had already laid Lily on his chair. With efficiency that he'd come to expect from her, Sara had the diaper off and was putting the new one on in no time. He took the wet diaper, rolled it up and placed it in the plastic bag he'd also taken from the diaper bag. He put it under the seat of the stroller. Sara was soon done dressing Lily again. Grant took his chair once more.

"Thank you, Judge. As I was saying…" As he finished Lily whimpered again. He took her from Sara and Lily quieted.

The judge looked at Sara. "Mrs. Smythe, do you have anything that you'd like to add?"

"Yes, I do."

Grant was a little surprised Sara was speaking up but the confidence in her voice gave him some.

"Lily had nobody and Grant took her. He had no experience with babies. In fact, he was a baby at taking care of a baby. But he has been a quick learner. As you can see, he has come a long way in a short time." Lily started to cry. She reached into the diaper bag and pulled out a burp pad. Handing it and a bottle to Grant, she continued, "This is one of the most caring and gentle men I've ever known. I'm sure the Armsteads are nice people and I'm sure they would do everything in their power to be good parents, but Grant and I both love Lily and think of her as our own. What you're seeing here between the three of us isn't for show. This is how it is. We're both involved in Lily's care. We are a partnership. Please let us continue to love and care for Lily."

By the sympathetic look and the nodding of the judge's

head Sara had made headway in their case to keep Lily. Trust her to speak so frankly and succinctly. Grant wanted her in his corner all the time. What would life have been like for him if he'd heard just a little of that confidence in him from his father? It didn't matter now because Sara had faith enough in him to make up for anything his father had said.

"Now, if you don't mind I think I'll take Lily outside to finish feeding her," Sara said.

The judge nodded. "That will be fine."

Sara pushed the stroller out of the way, stood and took Lily from Grant. The baby made a sound of protest. He quickly handed the bottle and rag to Sara, who smiled at him and left the room. The woman was a class act. Without her he wouldn't have had a chance to keep Lily.

Mr. Armstead sat forward in his chair. "Judge, I understand that Dr. Smythe and Mrs. Smythe have only been married a few weeks."

The judge looked at Grant. "Is this true?"

He needed to use as few words as possible. To always tell the truth. "Yes, sir."

"Did this custody case bring on a hasty marriage?"

"Sir, I consider marriage a serious institution. I would never enter into it without thought. I saw in Sara a wonderful mother. We both wanted to be parents to Lily. And we have been."

To Grant's great relief, the judge nodded as if satisfied.

"I think I have heard all I need. I'll let both parties know my decision in a week or two." The judge was clearly dismissing them.

Grant pushed the stroller out into the adjoining room and found Sara and Lily there. He took the now empty bottle from Sara and stored it away in the diaper bag. He spoke to Leon for a few minutes then they all walked to the parking area.

In the SUV, ready to go home, Grant turned to Sara. "Thanks. You were great in there. I'm grateful for all the nice things you said. I really think it made a difference."

She smiled. "I hope so. I meant every word. You have become and will continue to be a wonderful father."

"I hope the judge sees it that way."

"I'm sure he will."

Over the next week it was a waiting game. They didn't talk about the looming custody decision but Sara was well aware it weighed on Grant's mind. Still, those days were some of the happiest for her. She couldn't have wished for Grant to be more attentive. A number of times they went out to dinner but the dates were nowhere as extravagant as their first one. Even then the custody decision hung over their heads. If he won, would he expect her to leave right away? After all, that had been their agreement.

There were still no goodbye kisses when he left for work or returned. Not even during their dates, except for the one time when he'd presented her with a star named after her. It was as if he drew the line, equating that type of affection with a true marriage. Did he think if he kissed her in the light of day then theirs would no longer be a business deal? It was a daily reminder of the true nature of their relationship.

They talked, shared their life stories but he never said anything about how he felt about her. Neither did he question her about her feelings for him. They continued to play house as if nothing would ever change. Their time was sweet but she often wondered in the early hours of the morning when the bitter time would come. And it would, she was confident of that.

With each passing day her attachment to Lily grew as well. The baby who just ate and slept had grown into one who smiled and cooed at Grant and herself. With each passing day all that she feared was happening. Her love for Grant and Lily was deepening. There was nothing to stop the heartache now. The only thing she could do was try to survive it when the time came.

For someone outside, looking at her life, it couldn't be any better. For her, she was waiting for Grant to tell her to leave.

A week and a half after the court case Sara received a phone call from her former boss.

"Sara, I'm looking for someone to start up a program and oversee it in Wilmett. You were the first one to come to mind. I know the compassion you have for the patients and families and I understand your need to not get too involved right now. I thought this might be the perfect position for you. For the amount of work there will be a substantial salary." He told her an amount.

It was generous. "I'll have to think about it. I'm employed right now and I don't know how much longer this job will last."

"You're one of the best hospice nurses I've ever known. I really think you'll bring much-needed experience to the position. We would really like you to start as soon as possible. I hope you'll think about taking the job."

After discussing details of the job offer Sara pushed the disconnect button with a suddenly heavy heart. She'd known this day was coming but still wasn't prepared for it. The time had arrived for her to leave. She needed to do it before Grant had to tell her it was over. That didn't make her heart hurt any less. She was being given a job opportunity that she would normally snatch up but now with Lily and Grant...

But she had to go some time.

She would speak to Grant when he came in this evening. It wasn't a conversation she was looking forward to.

Grant came in not an hour later. She was at the sink and turned when the door opened. He entered with a smile on his face. Without stopping, he walked over and gathered her into a hug.

Her heart soared as she returned it. "Someone had a good day."

"I have." Grant stepped back. "Leon just called and said that we won the custody case. We need to celebrate."

We. There was no real we between them. There certainly wouldn't be after she told him her news. "That's wonderful. I'm so happy for you. You'll be a great father to Lily."

"I couldn't have done it without you."

"I'm glad I could help." She backed away.

He stared at her. "Is something wrong? I thought you'd be excited."

"I am. I'm really happy for you."

"You're not acting that way."

She put more space between them. "Well, it's just that the timing is interesting."

"How's that?" He no longer had a bright smile on his face.

She'd dreaded this with every fiber of her being but it had to be done. "I had a call from my old boss at the hospice service. He wants me to come back as part of a new program."

Grant didn't look pleased. "When?"

"Right away, if possible."

"You want to do that?" There was a hurt note in his voice.

"It's a manager's position. Those don't come along often."

"What about Lily? She needs you." More softly he said, "I need you."

"I appreciate that but we knew that this would come to an end one day soon."

By the stricken expression on his face he had no argument for that statement. "It'll take me time to get a replacement for you."

Sara was confident Grant would drag his feet about doing that. "You and I both know that you won't get a nanny until you're forced to do so. I recommend you call a service for help tomorrow. That way she and Lily will have a couple of days to get acquainted."

"Would it really be so bad to stay? I could match the pay."

That was equivalent to a slap in her face. "It's not about the money. It's about our agreement. It's time for me to go."

"Go?" He sounded like he'd never heard the word before.

"This was only to be temporary. You've not even been looking for another nanny."

"But I thought you were happy here."

She had been. Blissfully so. That was the problem. "It has been nice while it lasted but you knew I was only staying until the custody issue was settled. That's done now."

"I don't understand why you don't want to stay."

"I've been offered another job. This is the perfect time to leave." That was the wrong word. Nothing was perfect about the timing or the situation. But it was of her own making. Just like being a surrogate mother had been.

"Is this what you want?"

It wasn't about what she wanted. "It's the way it has to be. It's time for me to get back to my regular life. For you and Lily to find your lives together."

"We could do that with you."

"What's that supposed to mean?" Would he tell her how he felt? Did he trust her enough to share his life? She wanted it so badly but would it be best for them?

"I want you to stay."

"Why?"

He shifted from one foot to the other and looked anywhere but at her. "Because we're good together."

"Really? Why?"

Grant just stood there.

She sneered. "Oh, I get it. You get a nanny and a woman to warm your bed for the price of one. No, thanks."

He stepped toward her. "Don't put words in my mouth."

"Then what do you mean?"

"That you're great with Lily. We're great together."

"So let me get this right. Lily is well cared for and you are happy so I should stay?"

"I know for a fact you have been happy here." He gave her a wolfish grin.

She had been. The most contentment she'd ever known in her life was when she was in Grant's arms. That was the problem. She'd become too content. Had started to believe it was for real. It was going to hurt to leave him behind but it would cause more injury if she waited longer to leave.

"If I stayed, how long would it be for?" She shrugged her shoulder. "For two months? A year? Two? Until Lily is out of the house?"

"I don't know..." His words trailed off.

"Say I agree to stay another year. What will have changed? What happens when you meet someone you might be interested in?" Her chest tightened at the mere thought. "What if I do?"

He growled, "That won't happen."

"Who's to stop me?"

"I am."

"You're just my employer. This was a business agreement, Grant, not a marriage. I'm not your wife in the real sense of the word and I'm not Lily's mother."

He flinched. "What do you want? A real marriage?"

"You and I both know that you won't let your guard down enough for that to happen. You carry what your father and Evelyn did to you like a shield protecting you from any real relationship. Trust is the basis of any marriage. You're not willing to take the step to commit fully. To trust me with every part of your life. I get that, but it doesn't mean that I have to be willing to accept it. What I want is what is best for you and Lily. But I also have to think about myself."

"And that's to leave us?"

She stepped back until her butt touched the counter. "Yes. It's now or later. We both know it."

"So you're running, just like your mother did. Like you did after you had the baby. Now that you've got your father taken care of, you're out of here. To hell with Lily and me. You're betraying us."

"That's not true." He was hitting low now. Moisture filled her eyes. She squared her shoulders. "I am not."

"Yes, you are. You're running. I may need to learn to trust but how can I depend on someone who is always leaving?"

Was that what she was doing? "So what're you offering, Grant? For us to play house until you get unhappy or fall in love with another woman and tell me to get out?"

"That's not it at all."

"Do you really think we can have a real marriage where you and I live happily ever after?"

Grant's jaw twitched. Panic filled him. Sara was leaving. Everything he'd said to make her stay sounded weak and self-centered. What did he want from her? She wanted his love. He cared about her. Even wondered if he might be in love with her. But could he admit that and take the chance she would throw it back at him? She was all set to run.

"I don't know. But what I do know is that I don't want you to leave. Lily and I need you."

"What you need is to face your past. Accept that people are human and disappoint us. Have you ever thought that your father and Evelyn were both just selfish people who cared little for anyone but themselves? Or maybe Evelyn was a gold digger to begin with and used you to get to your father? You shouldn't let what they did define you, Grant. You're an amazing man who needs to learn to trust that someone can care for you. You need to face your demons and put them behind you."

Grant pulled in a deep breath. "And the woman who's running out on me is giving advice."

"You see me as leaving you. I'm not. We had an agreement. You got what you wanted. I did too. That's it plain and simple. It's time for me to go. I'm moving on."

"I doubt that. You're so compassionate that you'll find someone who needs help and you will become part of their life instead of living your own. Then you'll run again. You have already participated in two of life's largest events, having a baby and marriage, but neither one of those you did for yourself. You deserve to live for yourself. Stop running so you can have a life of your own."

"Grant, I think this conversation is over."

He was losing this battle. "And I think you expected things to be over before they even began."

"Bye, Grant."

The desire to spit nails filled him. How dared Sara walk out on him? He was better off without her. She was just like Evelyn. He'd started to care about her and here she was dumping him. They'd had their fun. It probably was time for her to go anyway.

So why did he feel pain larger and deeper than ever before? As if she'd just cut out his heart and taken it with her?

CHAPTER TEN

SARA BRUSHED AWAY the tears as she drove to her father's house. Her discussion with Grant, argument really, had been worse than she'd imagined. She'd said some ugly things. But he had as well. Some of it had needed to be said on both sides.

It hadn't taken her long to pack. Sara had touched the beautiful wedding dress that hung in the closet but hadn't folded it into her bag. She had taken the dresses Grant's mother had bought her. Before she'd left her and Grant's bedroom she'd pulled off her wedding ring. Biting her lower lip so she wouldn't cry, and with a shaking hand, she'd placed it on the bedside table.

Bag in hand, she'd stopped by Lily's room and looked in on her. She really was a perfect little girl. As wonderful as Emily. A tear had slid down Sara's face.

When Emily had emerged into the world, her friends Sally and Charles had been there, waiting to receive her. She herself had been an onlooker. The doctor had handed Emily over to them, not laid her on Sara's chest. Tears had crawled down her cheeks but she'd said they were from happiness for her friends. That wasn't true. They had come from the deep groaning heartache she'd felt at giving up something that had been a part of her. That time didn't compare to the misery she felt now at leaving Lily.

Grant. Just as it had had to be that way then, it had to be that way now. Would she ever stop having to give up people she loved? Would she ever be good enough for them?

She had found Grant in his father's den, sitting behind the desk.

"I'm leaving now."

He had looked up. "You know I want you to stay."

"And you know why I can't." It had hurt to say it but it was true.

"Thank you for all you have done for Lily."

"You're welcome. Did you find a nanny?" If he'd said no, would she have stayed for Lily's sake?

"I called a service. They're sending someone in the morning."

"You'll let me know when I need to sign the divorce papers."

"Sara..." The sentence had remained unfinished.

Their looks had met and held. Then she'd picked up her bag and walked out.

At her father's house she knocked on the front door. He answered with a look of surprise. "What're you doing here, little girl? And with your bag?"

"Dad, I need to tell you something."

"Come in," he said.

It felt odd, being invited into his home, because it had always been hers as well. Instead, she'd begun to think of Grant's as her home. Now she really didn't have one. She entered, placed her bag beside the door and followed her father into the sitting room.

"So what has happened, little girl?" her father asked as he settled into his chair.

She took the one nearby. "I'm sorry I couldn't tell you sooner but our marriage wasn't a real one. We only married so he could get custody of Lily."

"I suspected as much."

"He was awarded custody today."

"And you left." There was disapproval in his tone.

She nodded.

"I'd hoped you two could make it work. I could tell from the very beginning that there was something special between you. He's a good man. You can't work it out?"

"It's not to be, Dad."

Over the next few days she went about life in a daze. She started her new job but didn't have her heart in it. If she had a spare moment she wondered how Grant was doing, if the new nanny was taking care of Lily as she should. Sara was miserable. Sleep was hard to find. Focusing on work was sometimes impossible. And with each baby she saw she thought of Lily. Worse was the way her body ached for Grant's touch. As awful as she felt, it didn't help that her father looked at her with the pitiful expression of a man who didn't know what to do to make the situation better for someone he loved.

Time went by as slowly as a hot summer day and she questioned whether or not Grant was right. When she looked at it clearly and honestly she had to admit she had run. There was no doubt about that. But what if she had stayed? Maybe in time he would have been able to share his feelings. Grant was just getting adjusted to his new life as a single father. A lot had been thrown at him at once. Could she have remained if he had said he loved her? Her friends cared for her and would have welcomed her as a favorite aunt to Emily but she had run from them. She didn't want to run anymore. No longer push the good things in her life away.

Three weeks after leaving Grant, she and her father were having dinner when she blurted out, "Dad, why did Mother leave?"

"We've talked about this before."

"No, we haven't. I've asked and you've never answered. I'd like to know. Was it because of me?"

He looked grief-stricken. "Where did you get that idea?"

"You never would say. Is it because I'm too much like her?"

He took her hand. "Oh, little girl. It had nothing to do with you and everything to do with her. She always had a fragile personality. When she left it wasn't the first time. You just don't remember the others because you were too young. I would cover them up by saying she was visiting a friend. Your mother wasn't a happy person. She started taking drugs to make her feel better but that didn't work. I never wanted you to think badly of her so I thought it best you didn't know. As you grew older, you stopped asking."

"Do you know where she is?"

"The last I heard she was in a halfway house for drug addicts and not doing well. I think she left us because she loved us, not because she didn't. She just couldn't control her life. I'll never forgive her for the way she did it because she scared you. That was wrong. But what I do know is that she loved you dearly."

The moisture in her father's eyes matched that in Sara's.

"My greatest regret is that I couldn't have helped her more." He squeezed her hand. "You, Sara, are my true joy. You have cared for me, and more people than I can count as well. My fear isn't that you'll be like your mother but that you don't care enough about yourself.

"As your father, I say it's time for you to get out and live your life, not take care of me. Or anyone else, for that matter. You need to think of yourself for a change. Stop running from life and start living it. That big heart of yours is special but it can be your undoing."

Wasn't that what Grant had told her?

* * *

Later Sara sat in a chair on the deck, looking up at the night sky. Only a few weeks ago she would have never sat in the dark. She could only see a few stars but her heart warmed with the knowledge that there was a star named after her. Grant had given her more than she could have ever imagined. A place to belong, ease in the night, a child to care for, a home for her father and a taste of happiness beyond any she'd ever known.

She would make some changes. Starting with contacting her friends and seeing how they and their child, Emily, were doing. It was the first time she'd thought of her as belonging to them.

It was also time to figure out what she wanted out of life, then be prepared to grasp it and hold on.

Grant had been well aware of how much Sara had taken care of Lily and him but never more so than throughout the weeks since she had left.

There were no words enough to describe how much he missed her. He enjoyed sex as much as any red-blooded male but what he missed the most was having her against him in bed. More nights than not he prowled around the house then ended up sleeping on the couch.

He'd removed Evelyn's portrait from the living room, storing it away for Lily if she wanted it someday. He would adopt her when he could and would eventually tell her about her parents, leaving out the part where he was involved.

Looking around the den that he always thought of as his father's, he now saw it as his. It didn't hold the negative connotation it once had. One of last things Sara had done before she'd left had been to place on a bookshelf a framed photograph of him and Lily she'd taken.

Everywhere there were reminders of Sara. This den, in

the kitchen, Lily's room and the bedroom. She had permeated his life and found her way into his heart.

That hadn't happened before. But could he really trust Sara? He'd given what he'd believed was love before and had had it thrown back in his face. Could he take a chance of that happening again? It couldn't be any worse than the misery and loneliness he was living with now.

He looked out the window at the night sky. Even that reminded him of Sara. She was the strongest, most giving person he knew. Only she would carry a baby for someone and marry a man to save another. Wasn't that the type of person he could trust?

The phone rang and it was his mother. "I got your message that you won the custody case. Since that's what you wanted, I'm glad."

His mother might take some time but she would come around where Lily was concerned. It had taken him effort, with the help of Sara, and his mother would do the same, though sadly it would be with his assistance only.

"I did."

"You don't sound as excited as I thought you might be."

"I'm glad. It's just that now that has happened Sara has gone."

"I'm sorry to hear that." His mother did sound sorry. "Why?"

"Mother, she only agreed to marry me for Lily's sake and to help out her father."

"I don't believe that for a minute. Didn't you see the way she looked at you during the wedding? She cares about you. Quit letting your father and Evelyn's betrayal control your life."

"Why did he do it?" He didn't have to say his father's name.

"Because he was a self-centered old man who let his vanity hurt someone he loved very much."

"He didn't love me."

"Yes, he did. He just didn't know how to show it. You were everything he had wanted to be and couldn't be any more. He was a weak man, jealous of your youth, your abilities, your girlfriends, and your intellect. But that didn't mean he didn't love you. I know that you don't remember because they were covered by ugliness as you got older, but he was a good father at one time. It could have been him or us both who made you see love with such a distrustful view. I'm sorry for that."

"Mom, you didn't—"

"Don't start lying to me now. Just know that there are good people out there who will not disappoint you. Take a chance. Figure out some way to make peace with what your father did and find happiness. I have to go. I'll call again soon." She hung up.

How like his mother to drop a bombshell and move on. How was he supposed to find peace?

He spent the next few weeks asking himself that question daily and coming up with no answer. Sara would know what he needed to do. He picked up the phone to call her but ended up putting it down more than once. She'd made her position clear. He had to respect that. Between looking for a way to find peace, missing Sara and dealing with the demanding replacement nanny, he was at his stress max. His colleagues seemed to find somewhere else they were needed when he came around. He wasn't a fun person. He'd liked who he was around Sara.

Two nights later, on his way home from the hospital, he passed the lot where his father had taken him as a child to look at the stars. An office building had been built on the lot but he pulled into the parking area and turned off the engine. Stepping out, he looked up at the sky. He couldn't see the stars as clearly as he had as a boy but they were there.

His father had given him the love of stargazing, something that Grant was sure to pass on to Lily. So how had things turned so ugly between him and his father?

"What did I do, Dad? Why did you treat me the way you did?"

There was no answer, only the sound of a distant car along the street.

Grant shook his fist at the sky. "Why would you treat someone you loved the way you did?"

His chest tightened. Was he holding his father to a higher standard than he himself could live up to? Hadn't he also pushed someone he cared about away? Had his father been hurt by *him*? His mother? Brother? His father was human. Everyone had feelings. He'd never thought of his father as a man with fears, faults and foibles.

What he needed to do was not make the same mistakes. It should be his goal to see that Lily grew up safe and secure. To know she was loved and valued.

She'd had that with him and Sara. But Sara was no longer in their lives. He'd never trusted her enough to ask her to stay. Why had he treated Sara the way he had? Why hadn't he been able to tell her he loved her? He did.

Because he was scared. He didn't want to feel the pain of rejection as he had with his father. Evelyn. But wasn't he in pain anyway? How much more agony would he have if he ignored how he felt about Sara? Tried to go thought life without her? He groaned.

He'd remember the lessons of his past, change his present and strive for a happy future. The first step in doing those was to talk to Sara and beg, plead and promise her all the love he could give.

* * *

Sara was in the process of dressing for the day after another fitful night of sleep when her phone rang. It was Kim.

They had been in touch since her and Grant's breakup. Sara had explained that it just hadn't worked out between her and Grant.

Kim's retort had been, "You sure looked like you were getting along fine at the wedding."

Sara had responded with a few more noncommittal statements and after that Kim had let the discussion drop.

To hear from her so early in the morning to mean something was wrong. Her heart thumped against her chest. Was it Grant?

"I thought you would want to know. Lily's been admitted to the hospital."

Sara sank to the bed. "What happened?"

"I'm not sure. I just know that Grant canceled all his cases for the next few days."

"I'm on my way. Thanks for letting me know."

Sara, with heart pounding and gripping the steering wheel, pulled into the hospital parking lot just before eight. Why hadn't Grant called her? Then again, why would he? After all, she'd left acting as if she wanted nothing more to do with him or Lily. But loved them dearly and wanted nothing more than to be a part of their lives. Even if her and Grant's relationship was rocky, she could still show concern for Lily. Maybe help.

There were so many diseases that could cause a young child to become sick. Ones that could affect Lily for the rest of her life. Trying not to think the worst, she hurried through the double sliding glass doors into the lobby of the huge metropolitan hospital. She stopped at the reception desk and gave Lily's name.

The middle-aged woman told her a floor and room number. "Only immediate family are allowed at this hour."

"I'm Mrs. Smythe." It was the first time she'd used the title in public. She found it rolled off her lips rather easily, as if it belonged. At the bank of elevators, she entered one and rode up.

She hesitated before walking down the long tiled hallway. Would Grant be glad to see her? What would she do if he sent her away? She couldn't let those worries stop her. He needed her even if he didn't think he did.

Sara knocked quietly on the door to the room then pushed it open. No one stirred. "Grant?" she said softly, not to wake Lily if she was asleep. Sara stepped further into the room. What she found broke her heart.

Grant sat on a small sofa with his head in his hands. She'd seen him angry, disillusioned, and sad, but nothing like the total despondency she was witnessing now. Looking around the room, she didn't see Lily. *Oh, no!*

"Grant?"

He looked at her, sat up straighter. His arms opened and she walked into them. Sitting on one of his knees, Sara wrapped her arms around his neck and held him tight. Grant put his head in her chest. They sat like that for a few minutes. He finally looked at her. His eyes were red-rimmed from tiredness or emotion, she wasn't sure which.

"Lily?"

"The doctor thinks she has meningitis. They have taken her down for a spinal tap."

Relief flooded her. Thank goodness it wasn't the worst, as she'd feared.

"They don't know if it's viral or bacterial. She's so sick. Running a fever, crying so that nothing makes her happy.

I've seen many sick adults but nothing as pitiful as Lily. I was helpless to do anything for her."

"We just have to believe that she'll be fine." Sara rubbed his back.

"I came home very late this morning and the nanny met me at the door, frantic. I took one look at Lily and knew we needed to get to the hospital as soon as possible. Do you know what it's like to have to hand over someone you love to someone else to care for? I felt powerless."

Her chest constricted. "I know exactly what you mean."

His gaze met hers. "I'm sorry, I guess you do. Better than most."

"How long has Lily been gone?"

"About thirty minutes. They said it would take about an hour."

Sara untangled herself from him. "You need some rest. If I understand correctly, you haven't had any in over twenty-four hours. Get some sleep so you can think straight."

"I need to wait to hear what they say about Lily."

She stood. "I'm not going anywhere. I'll wake you when she comes back."

Grant took her hand. "Sit with me. I've missed you."

Sara nodded and took a seat at the far end of the sofa. "Put you head in my lap and close your eyes."

He leaned back and did as he was told. "That's what I missed most about you being gone. Someone taking care of me," he murmured as his eyelids lowered.

Grant's large body crammed on the small sofa reminded her of too many circus clowns trying to get into a tiny car. Seemingly impossible but accomplished. Sara stroked his hair and soon he was breathing evenly. She'd be here as long as he needed her. Until he told her to go. No more running.

* * *

Grant woke to the sound of Sara's voice. She was there with him. He'd never been so glad to see someone.

Lily. What about Lily?

He sat up. A nurse and an orderly were positioning Lily's metal baby bed against the far wall. Sara stood and started across the space. Her posture implied she was in caregiver mode. He joined her beside Lily, who lay quietly in the bed.

"What did they find out?" Sara asked the nurse as she brushed a finger across Lily's cheek.

"The doctor will be in to speak to you in a few minutes," the nurse said, straightening out an IV line. She and the orderly nodded before they left.

"I don't think I've ever been more scared than I have been in the last few hours." Grant gripped the bed. "To think I resented Lily, offloaded my issues with our father on her."

Sara rubbed a hand across his shoulders as they both looked down at the child. "You came around pretty quickly. It doesn't take long to fall in love with her."

"Yeah, but I didn't do as well by you." He put an arm around her waist.

Her body tensed.

Was Sara afraid of what he might say next? "I love you, Sara. I think I have since the moment I saw you in the door of the chapel. Whatever happens here, I still want you with me. We belong together."

She turned in his arms and before she could say anything his lips found hers.

Someone cleared their throat. Grant pulled back. He glanced around and saw Lily's doctor. Releasing Sara, Grant took a step toward the balding man in scrubs with a lab coat over them. "Dr. Rodgers, what did you find out?"

He smiled. "The preliminary test shows no bacterial meningitis."

"That's great." Grant turned and hugged Sara briefly. She had tears in her eyes. Keeping a hand at her waist, he presented her to the doctor. "This is my wife, Sara."

"Nice to meet you," Dr. Rodgers said.

"So what happens now?" Grant asked.

"Lily will need to at least stay overnight and we'll start antibiotics and keep her on fluids just to be on the safe side. She should be able to go home tomorrow if there are no negative changes."

Grant shook hands with him. "Thank you so much."

"You're welcome. Now, why don't you try to get some rest? You look like you need it." With a smile he left the room.

Grant gathered Sara into his arms again for a tight hug. She returned it. When he let go he cupped her face and looked into her eyes. "Tell me you won't ever leave me again."

She smiled. His heart almost beat out of his chest. "I love you too and I'm never leaving you and Lily again."

"That's what I wanted to hear." He found her lips again.

Lily whimpered. Sara broke their kiss. Reaching into the bed, she picked up Lily and cradled her against her chest. There was a rocker in the room and Sara sat in it. Grant adjusted the IV pole so it stood nearby. Sara looked down into Lily's face. "I've missed you, my little love."

Grant's world had righted itself.

Sara couldn't believe that Grant had said that he loved her. Even more significant was that he'd kissed her right there in the hospital room. Even more wonderful, it was the first of many times he did so.

She talked Grant into going home only by reassuring

him she wouldn't leave Lily for a minute. Hoping he would stay and get some rest, she really wasn't surprised when he turned up hours later with food for both of them. They stayed the night in Lily's room, taking turns sleeping on the sofa. Lily was released the next morning. Sara called work, saying she wouldn't be in, and followed Grant and Lily home.

As she pulled up the drive she thought back to that first meeting between her and Grant. She chuckled. They had come a long way since then. Circling the house, she took her old slot in the carport. Grant had Lily out of the car seat by the time she arrived to help him. She had missed these moments and had believed she'd never have them again.

An hour later they had Lily fed and settled in her bed for a nap. They each placed a kiss on her forehead. Out in the hall, Grant said, "As much as I would like a nap myself, with you naked beside me, I think we need to talk first. Then, as your doctor, I'm going to order one."

He took her hand and led her down to the kitchen. She broke their contact. "I'll fix you some coffee and put on water for tea."

Grant took a seat at the table. As she worked she felt him watching her.

"You know, after you left I hated coming in here almost as much as I had hated going into my father's den. This is just a kitchen when you aren't here but when you are it becomes a home."

She looked at him. "Thank you. That might be the nicest compliment I've ever been given."

"I meant every word. Sara, I'm sorry I couldn't see what was right in front of me. I was so scared to trust you or anyone else again that I almost lost you."

"So what happened to change your mind?"

"You leaving. Me being miserable. Being forced to face

my demons. I had to accept my father was human. He made mistakes but they weren't ones I have to repeat. I could lose the best thing that ever happened to me or decide that I would be different. I've chosen different."

She brought him a mug of coffee and set her cup and saucer on the table. "I've known you were different from the moment you decided to raise Lily."

"Sara, I want you to help me do that." He put his hand in his pocket, pulling out her wedding ring. Going down on one knee, he took her left hand. "Will you continue to be my wife?"

Joy surged through her. He slipped the ring on her finger. She kissed him with all the love in her heart. Breathless, she broke the kiss. This was her time and she was going to grasp it and hold on for dear life.

Grant sat in his chair again but didn't let go of her hand.

"I'd like to tell you something."

"Anything." He kissed her hand.

"I called Emily's parents."

Grant looked at her intently. "How did that go?"

"Better than I thought it would. I cried. They cried. And they forgave me. I'm planning to have dinner with them next week. Would you go with me?"

He smiled. "Just try to stop me."

"I have one more request."

"Name it and it's yours."

She looked at his handsome sincere face that she loved so much. "Will you call me sweetheart?"

His smile reached his eyes. "I will every day for the rest of our lives, sweetheart."

* * * * *

MILLS & BOON®
Hardback – May 2016

ROMANCE

Morelli's Mistress	Anne Mather
A Tycoon to Be Reckoned With	Julia James
Billionaire Without a Past	Carol Marinelli
The Shock Cassano Baby	Andie Brock
The Most Scandalous Ravensdale	Melanie Milburne
The Sheikh's Last Mistress	Rachael Thomas
Claiming the Royal Innocent	Jennifer Hayward
Kept at the Argentine's Command	Lucy Ellis
The Billionaire Who Saw Her Beauty	Rebecca Winters
In the Boss's Castle	Jessica Gilmore
One Week with the French Tycoon	Christy McKellen
Rafael's Contract Bride	Nina Milne
Tempted by Hollywood's Top Doc	Louisa George
Perfect Rivals...	Amy Ruttan
English Rose in the Outback	Lucy Clark
A Family for Chloe	Lucy Clark
The Doctor's Baby Secret	Scarlet Wilson
Married for the Boss's Baby	Susan Carlisle
Twins for the Texan	Charlene Sands
Secret Baby Scandal	Joanne Rock